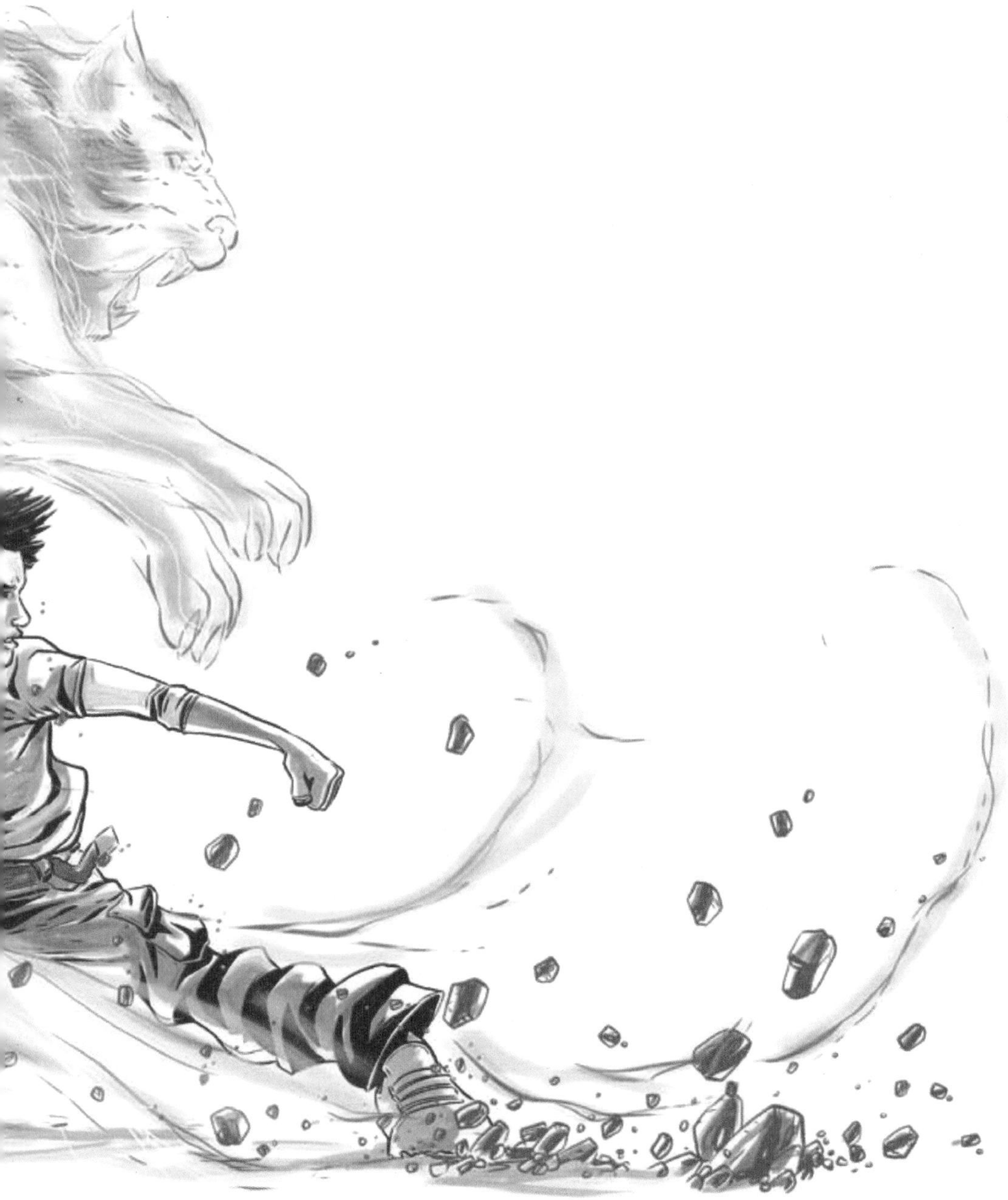

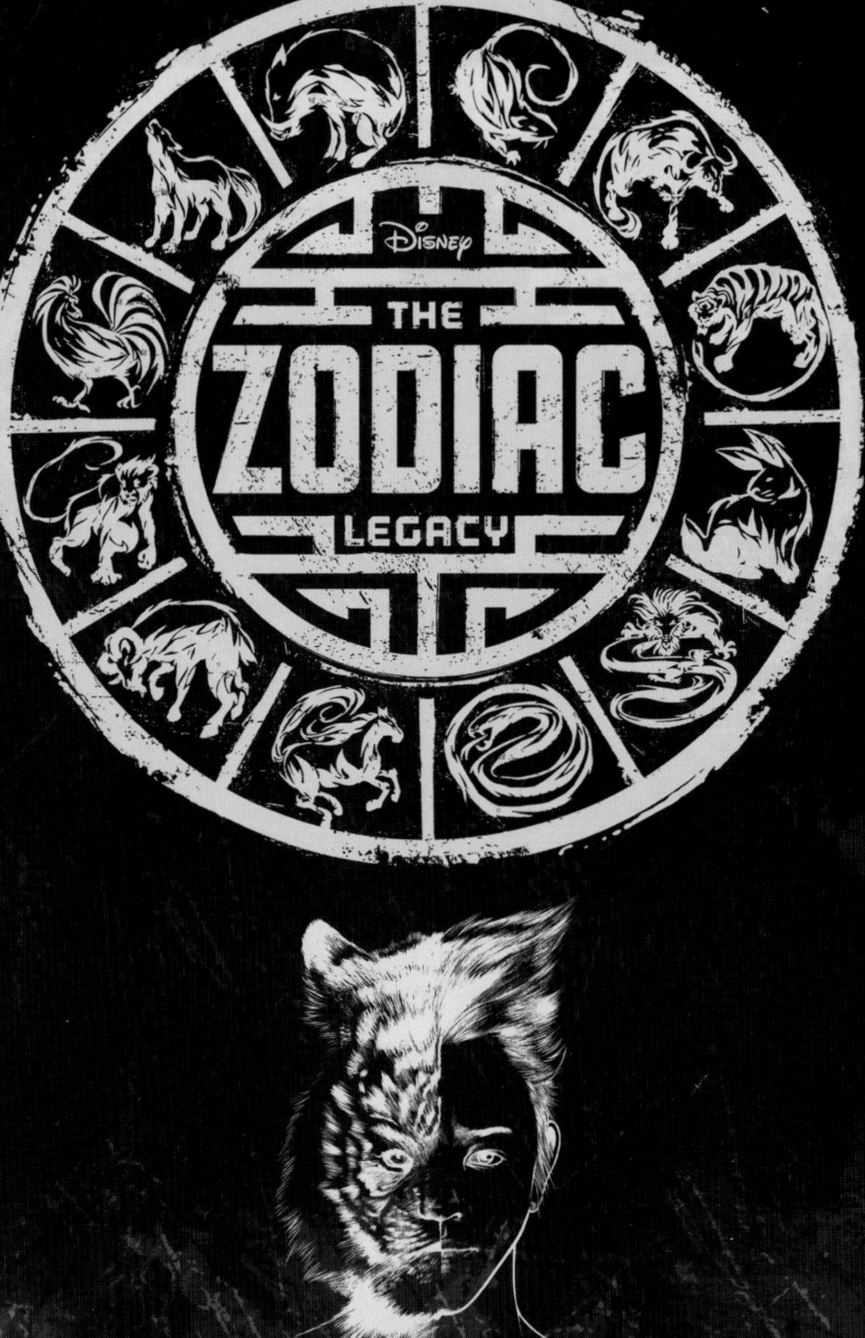
Disney
THE
ZODIAC
LEGACY

PAPERCUTZ

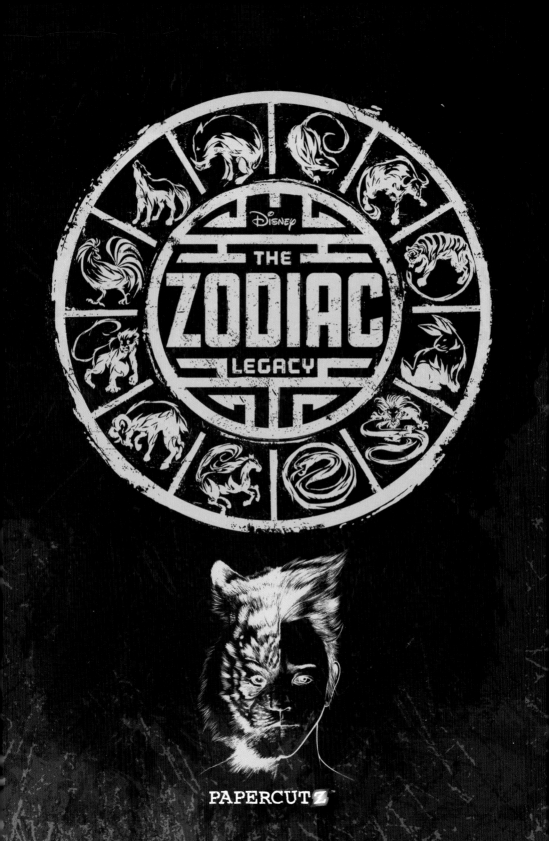

Disney Graphic Novels available from PAPERCUTZ

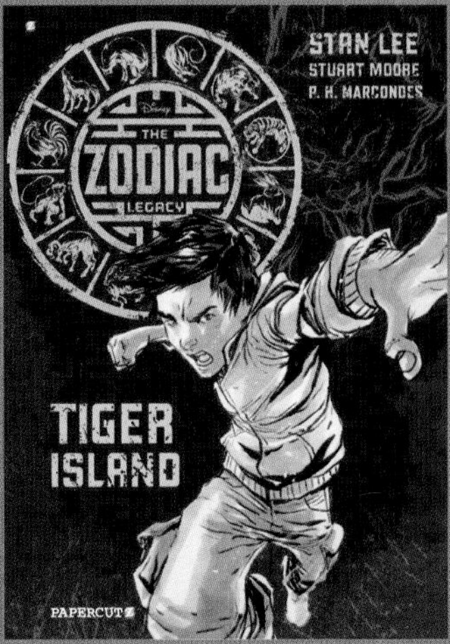
STAN LEE
STUART MOORE
P. H. MARCONDES
THE ZODIAC LEGACY
TIGER ISLAND
PAPERCUTZ

DISNEY THE ZODIAC LEGACY

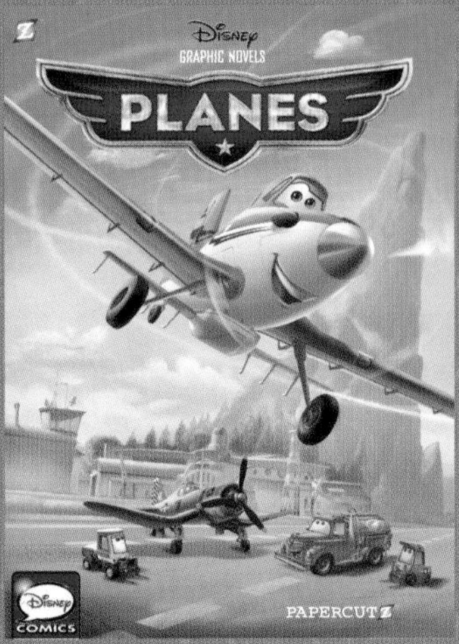
Disney
GRAPHIC NOVELS
PLANES
Disney COMICS
PAPERCUTZ

DISNEY PLANES

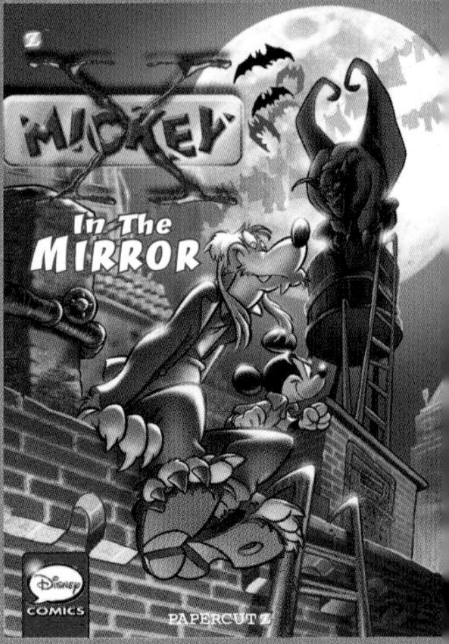
X-MICKEY
In The MIRROR
Disney COMICS
PAPERCUTZ

DISNEY X-MICKEY

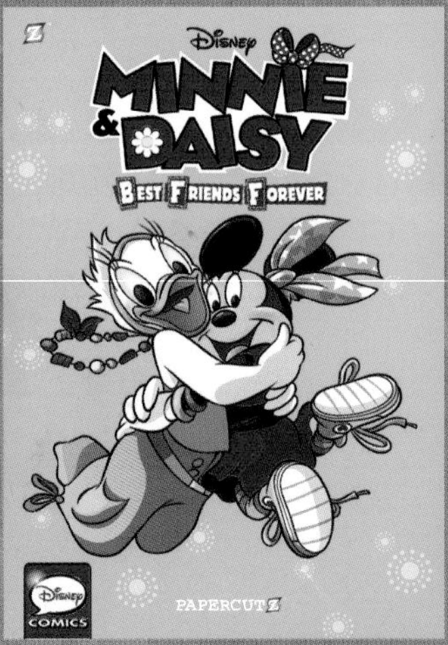
Disney
MINNIE & DAISY
BEST FRIENDS FOREVER
Disney COMICS
PAPERCUTZ

DISNEY MINNIE & DAISY BFF

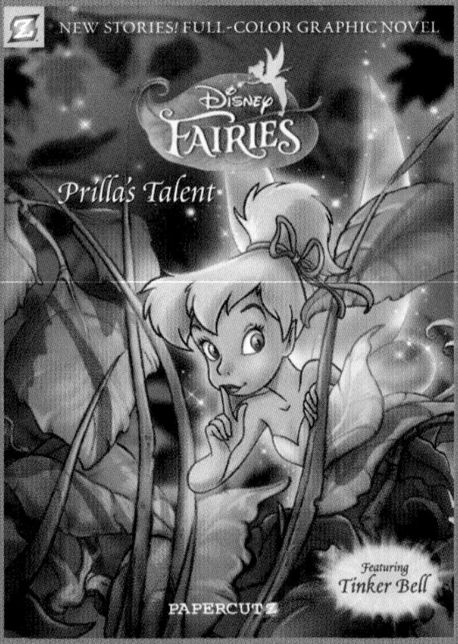
NEW STORIES! FULL-COLOR GRAPHIC NOVEL
Disney FAIRIES
Prilla's Talent
Featuring Tinker Bell
PAPERCUTZ

DISNEY FAIRIES #1

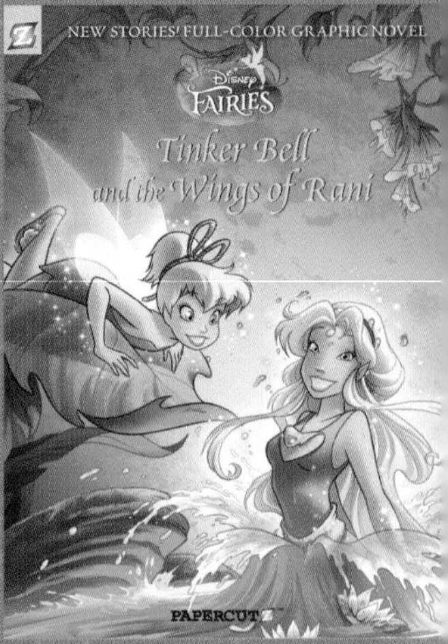
NEW STORIES! FULL-COLOR GRAPHIC NOVEL
Disney FAIRIES
Tinker Bell and the Wings of Rani
PAPERCUTZ

DISNEY FAIRIES #2

Disney graphic novels are available in paperback for $7.99 each; in hardcover for $12.99 each. Available a booksellers everywhere. Or you can order from us: Please add $4.00 for postage and handling for first book and add $1.00 for each additional book. Please make check payable to NBM Publishing. Send to: Papercutz, 160 Broadway, Suite 700, East Wing, New York, NY 10038 or call 800-886-1223 (9-6 EST M-F) MC-Visa-Amex accepted

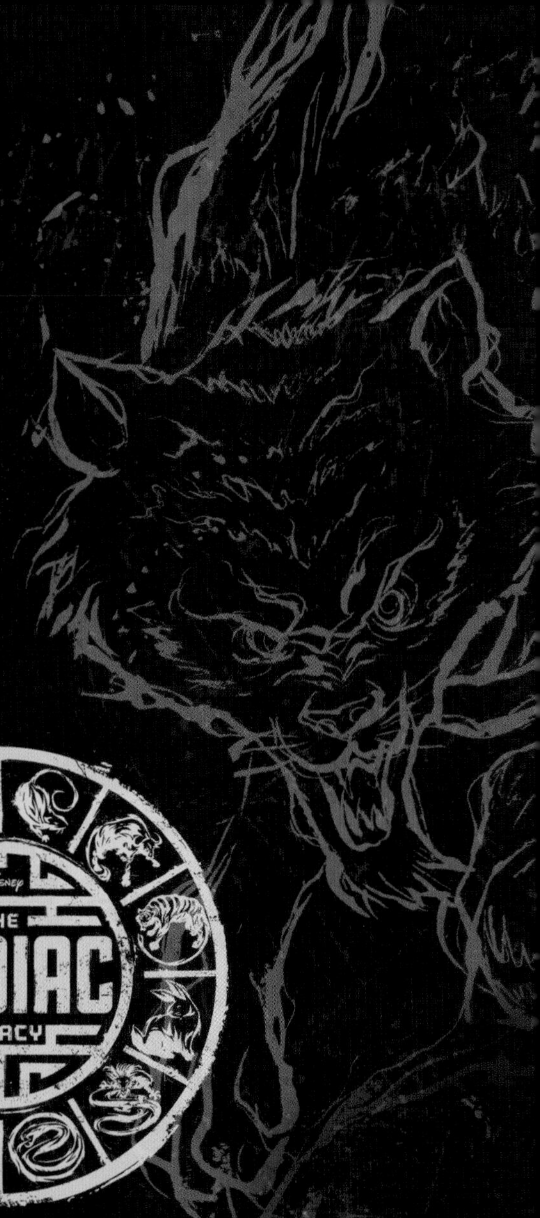

The Zodiac Legacy

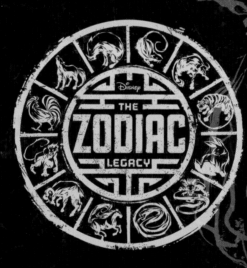

#1 "Tiger Island"

Stan Lee – Creator

Stuart Moore – Writer

P.H. Marcondes – Artist

PAPERCUTZ

New York

#1 "Tiger Island"
Stuart Moore — Writer
P.H. Marcondes — Artist
Andie Tong — Cover, Endpapers, and Character Profiles Artist
Jolyon Yates — Title Page Artist
Jay Jay Jackson — Character Color Design
Matteo Baldrighi — Colorist
Roberta Marchetta
Paola Selene Fiorino
Giovanni Spadaro — Color Assistants
Salvatore Di Marco (Grafimated) — Color Assistants Coordinator
Bryan Senka — Letterer
Dawn Guzzo — Production
Brittanie Black — Production Coordinator
Jeff Whitman — Assistant Managing Editor
Jim Salicrup
Editor-in-Chief

ISBN: 978-1-62991-296-7 paperback edition
ISBN: 978-1-62991-297-4 hardcover edition

Papercutz books may be purchased for business or promotional use. For information on bulk purchases
please contact Macmillan Corporate and Premium Sales Department at (800) 221-7945 x5442.

Printed in Korea through Four Colour Print Group
June 2016 by WE SP Co., Ltd.
79-29 Soraji-ro, Paju-Si
Gyeonggi-do, Korea 10863

Distributed by Macmillan
First Printing

The power of the Zodiac comes from twelve pools of mystical energy.

Due to a sabotaged experiment, twelve magical superpowers are unleashed on Steven Lee and twelve others.

Now Steven Lee is thrown into the middle of an epic global chase.

He'll have to master strange powers, outrun super-powered mercenaries, and unlock the secrets of the Zodiac Legacy. When Steven is first rescued by Jasmine and Carlos, he relishes his newfound powers and is excited to be on a grand adventure, alongside...

TIGER

STEVEN

POWERS:
STRENGTH, REFLEXES

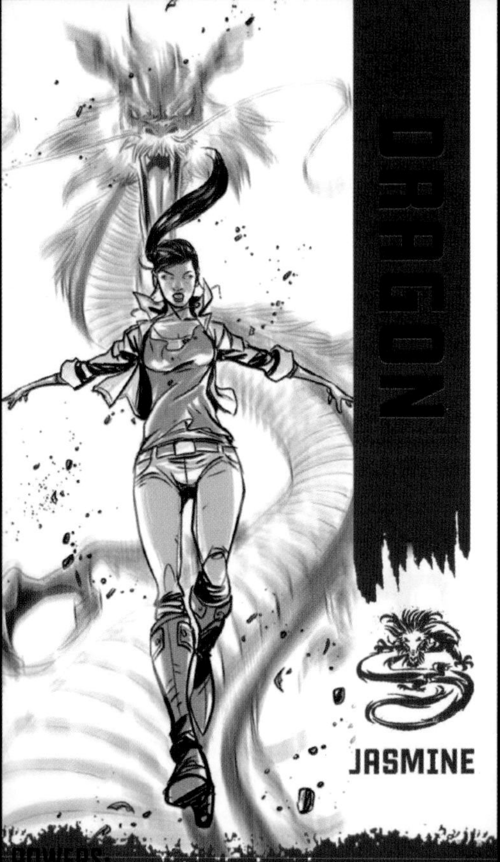
DRAGON
JASMINE

POWERS:

FIRE BREATHING, FLIGHT,
MIND CONTROL

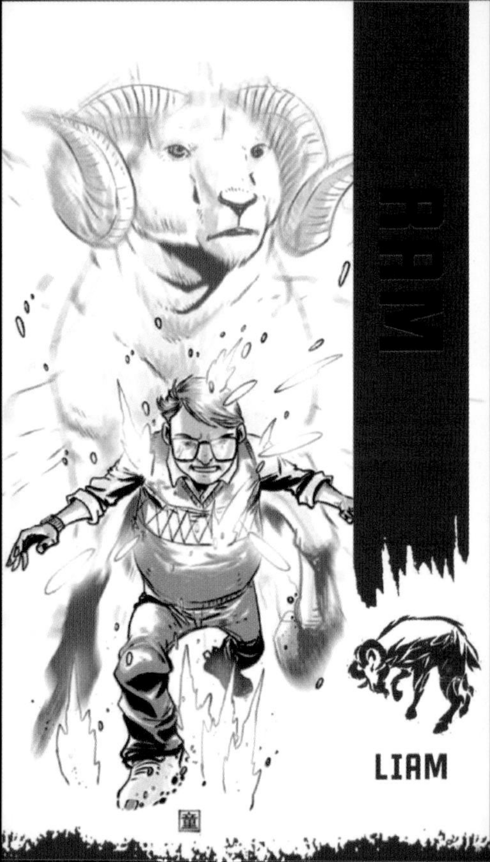
RAM
LIAM

POWERS:

INVULNERABILITY

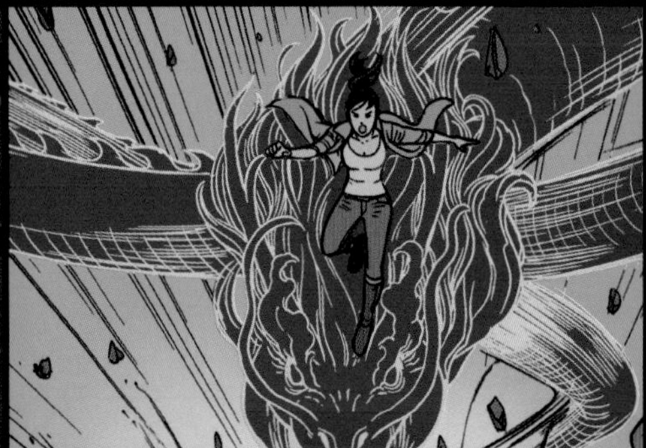

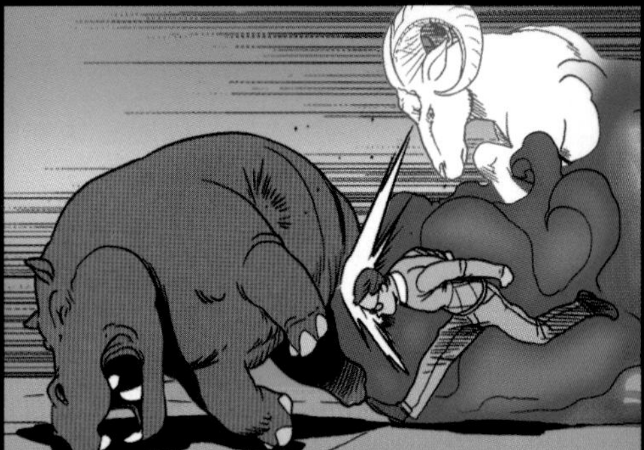

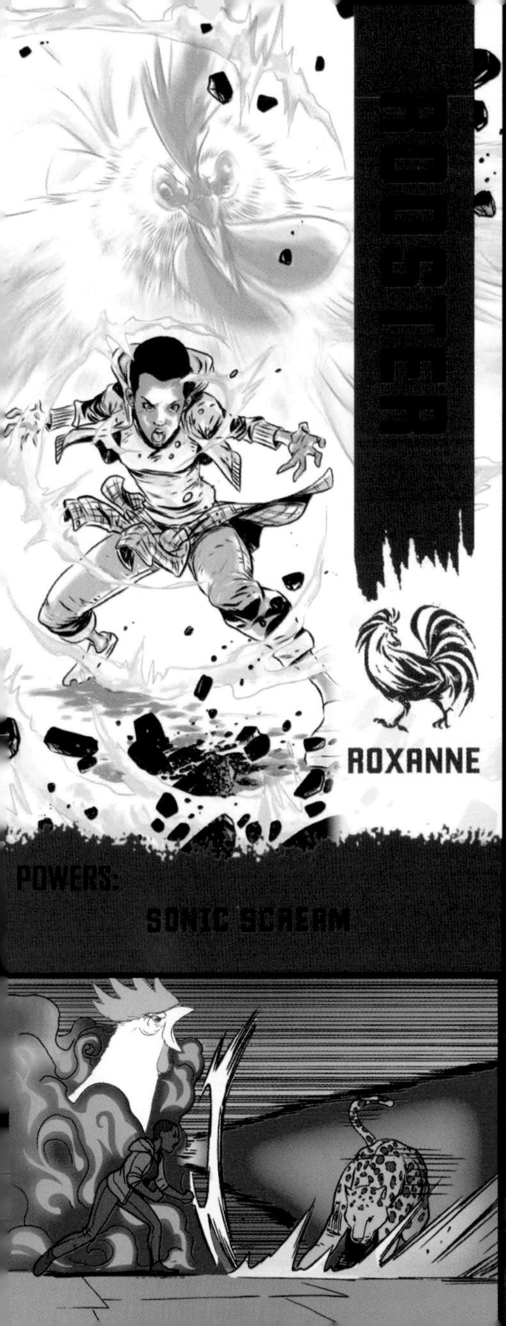
ROOSTER
ROXANNE
POWERS:
SONIC SCREAM

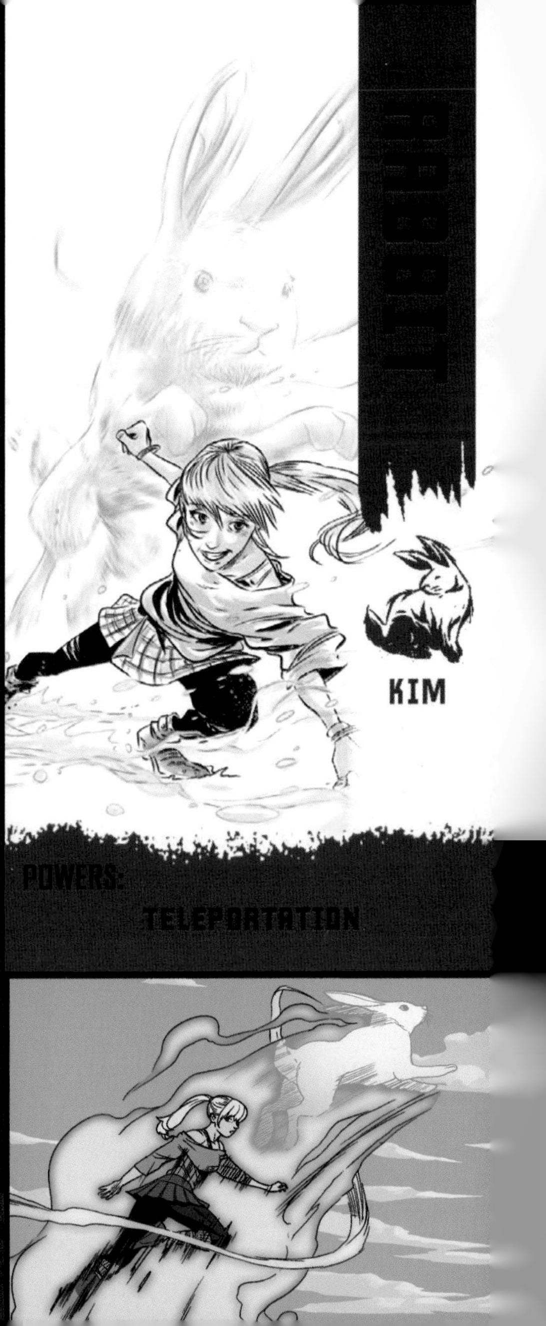
RABBIT
KIM
POWERS:
TELEPORTATION

PIG

DUANE

POWERS:

INFORMATION PROCESSING

Steven and his
new friends will
need to stay one
step ahead of the
Vanguard...

DRAGON

MAXWELL

POWERS:
FIRE BREATHING, FLIGHT,
MIND CONTROL

The Vanguard organization is bent on tracking down all of the Zodiac powers. The Vanguard are...

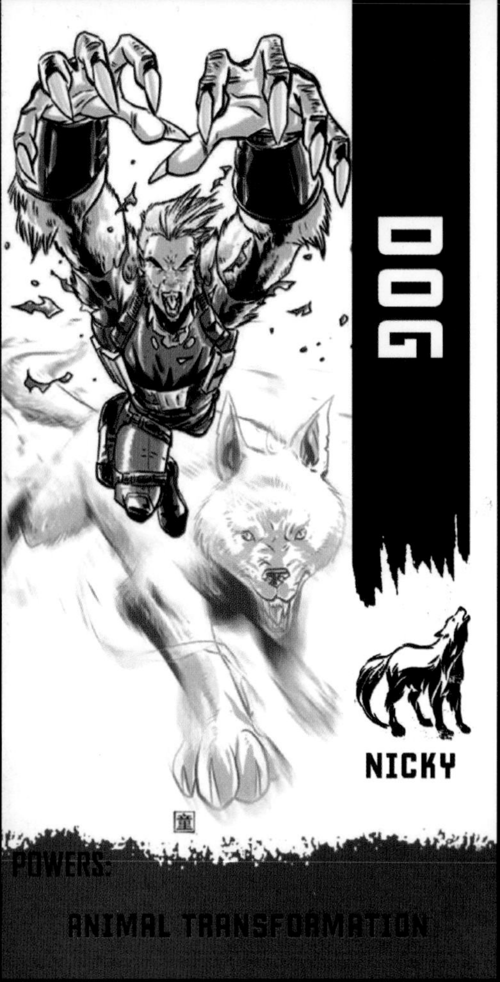
DOG
NICKY
POWERS:
ANIMAL TRANSFORMATION

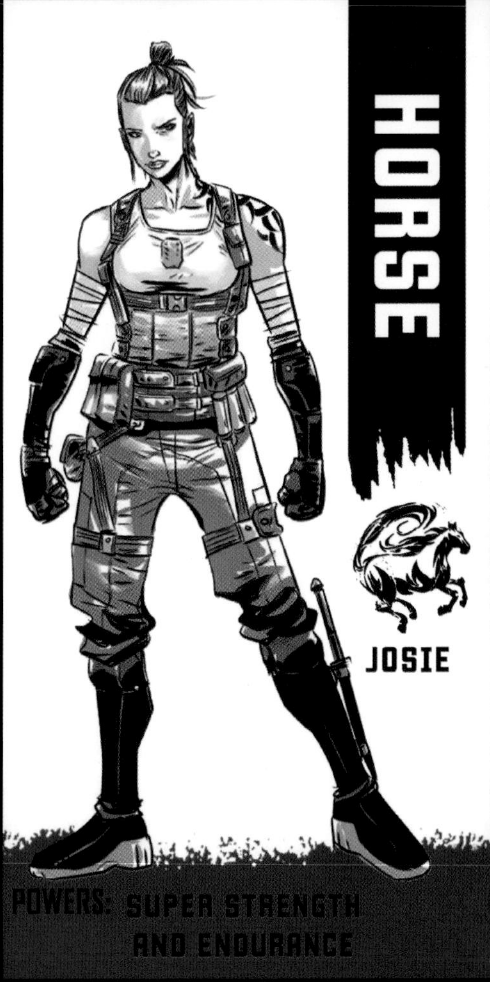
HORSE
JOSIE
POWERS: SUPER STRENGTH
AND ENDURANCE

DOG

狗

HORSE

馬

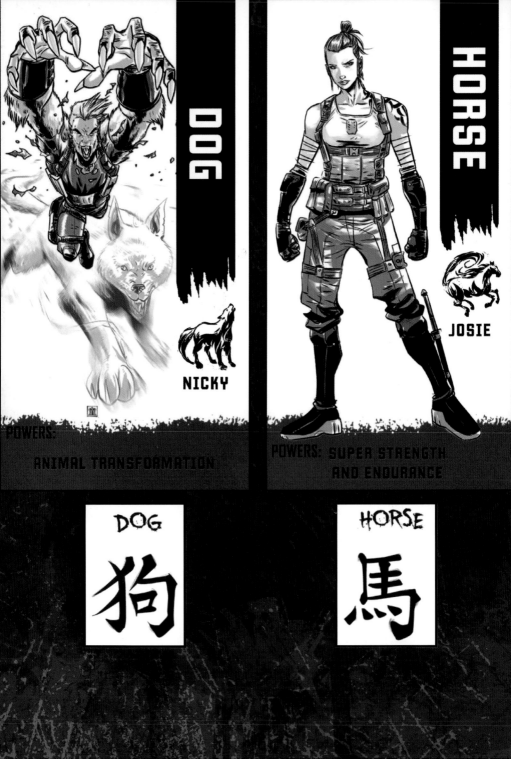

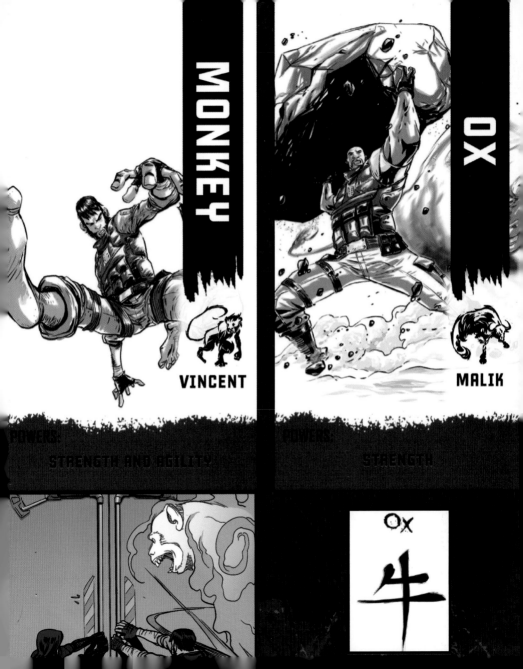

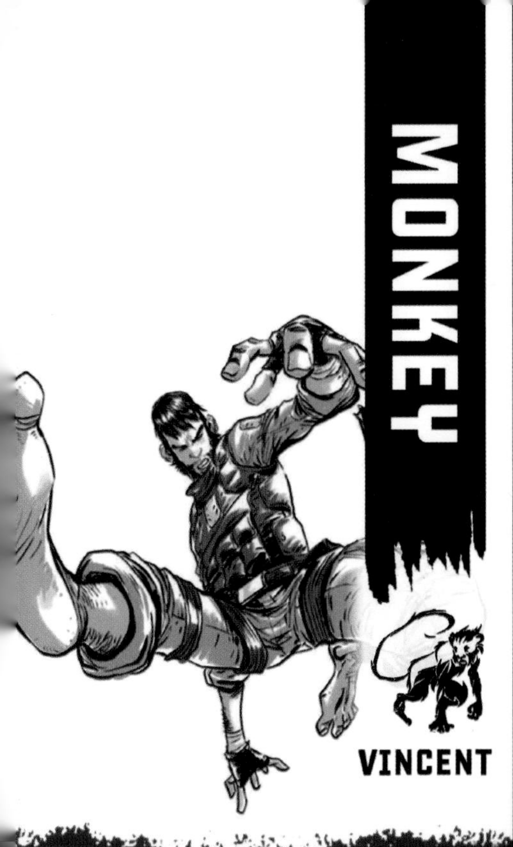
MONKEY
VINCENT

POWERS:

STRENGTH AND AGILITY

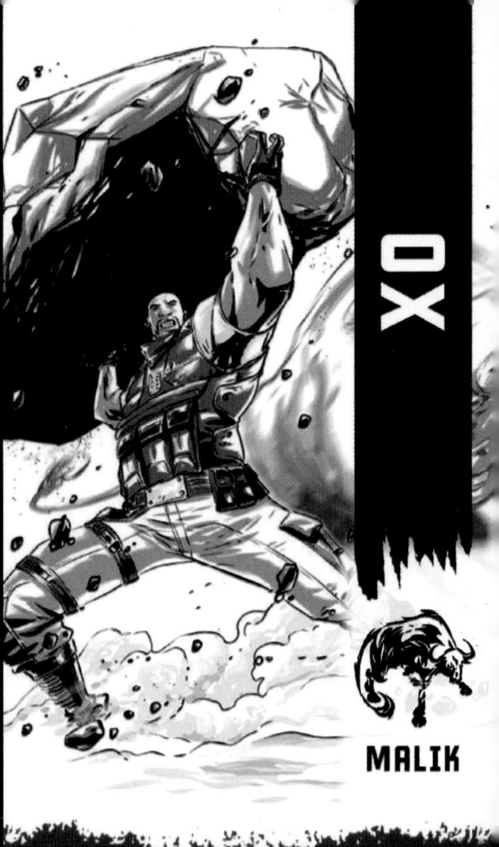
OX
MALIK

POWERS:

STRENGTH

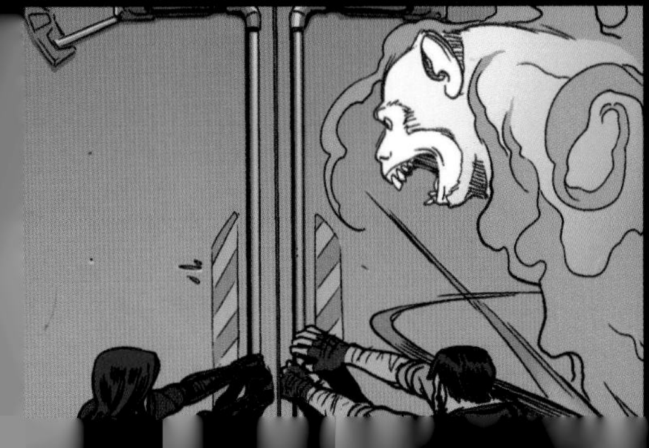

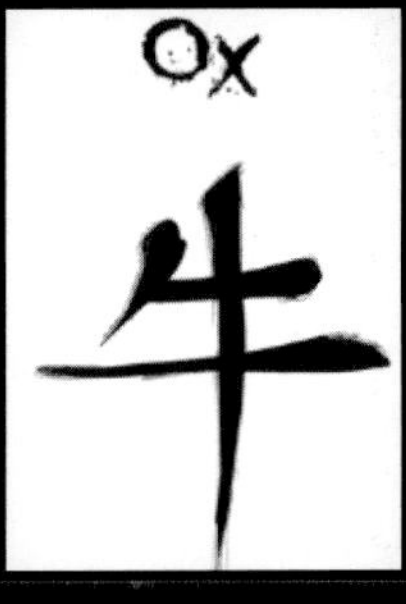
Ox
牛

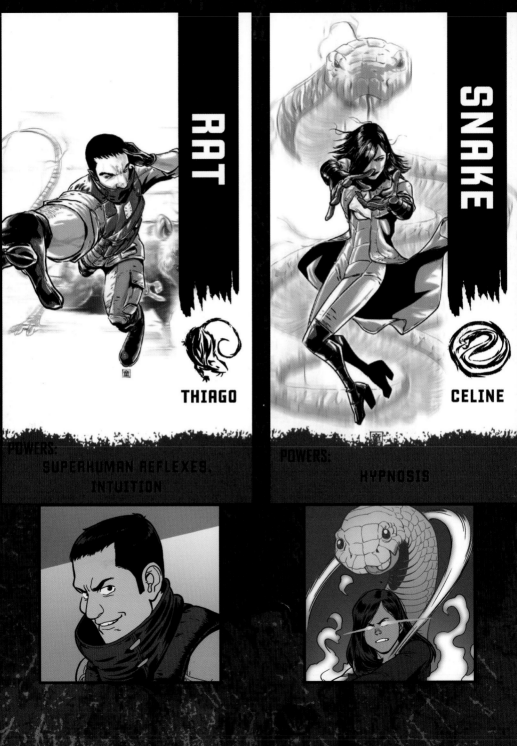

RAT

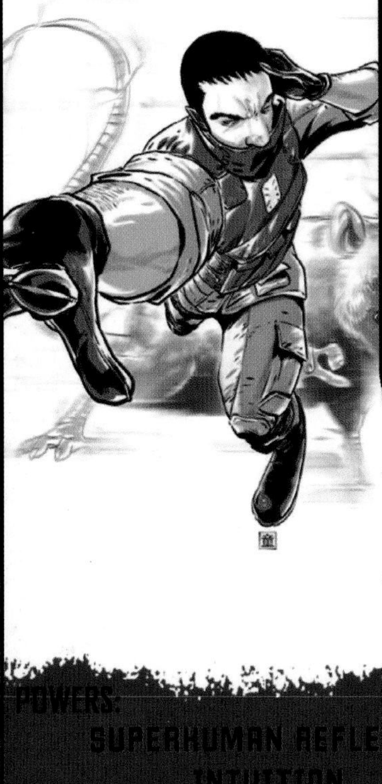

THIAGO

POWERS:
SUPERHUMAN REFLEXES, INTUITION

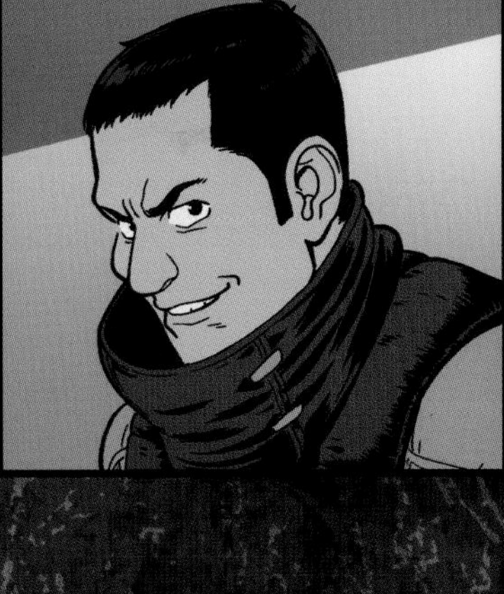

SNAKE

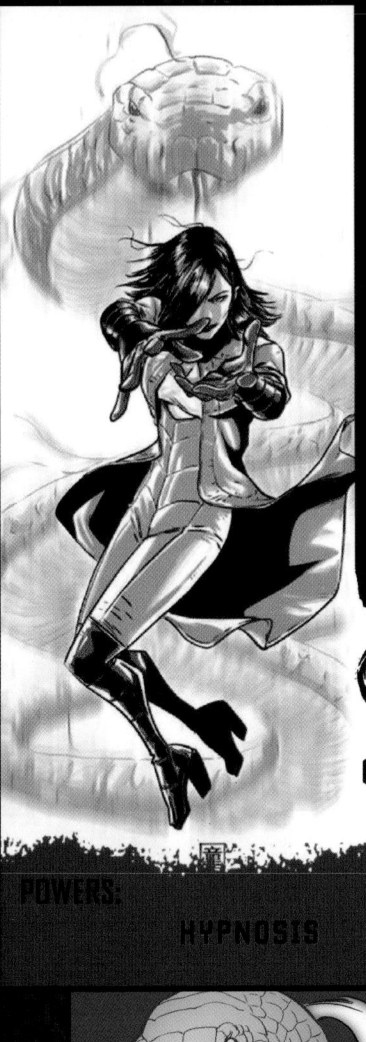

CELINE

POWERS:
HYPNOSIS

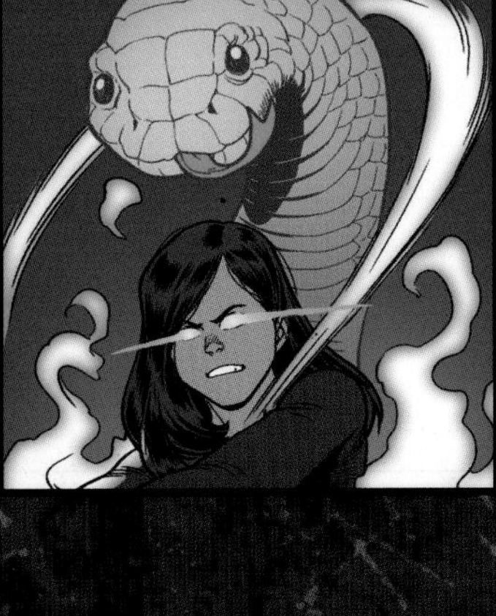

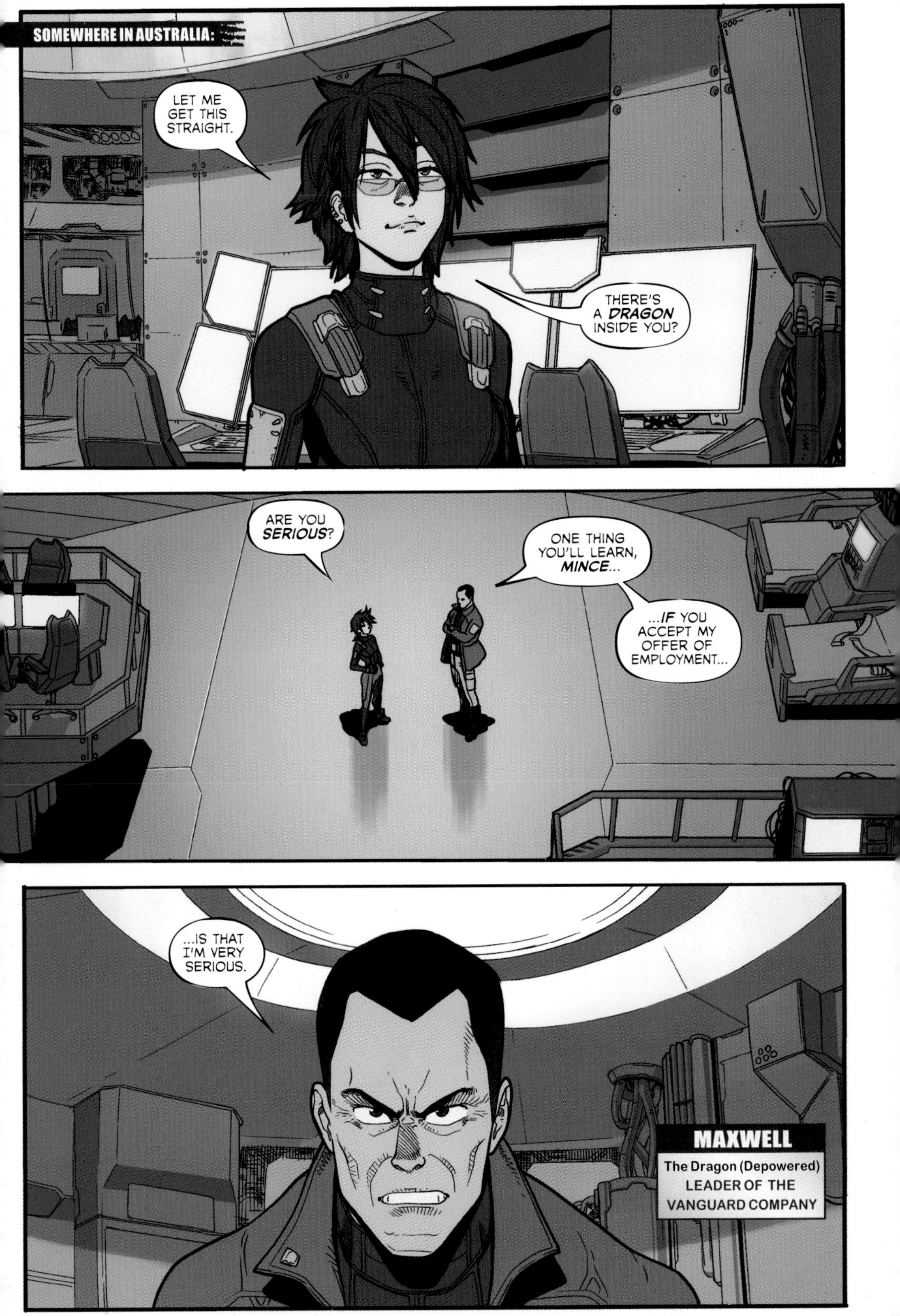
SOMEWHERE IN AUSTRALIA:
LET ME GET THIS STRAIGHT.
THERE'S A DRAGON INSIDE YOU?
ARE YOU SERIOUS?
ONE THING YOU'LL LEARN, MINCE...
...IF YOU ACCEPT MY OFFER OF EMPLOYMENT...
...IS THAT I'M VERY SERIOUS.
MAXWELL
The Dragon (Depowered)
LEADER OF THE VANGUARD COMPANY

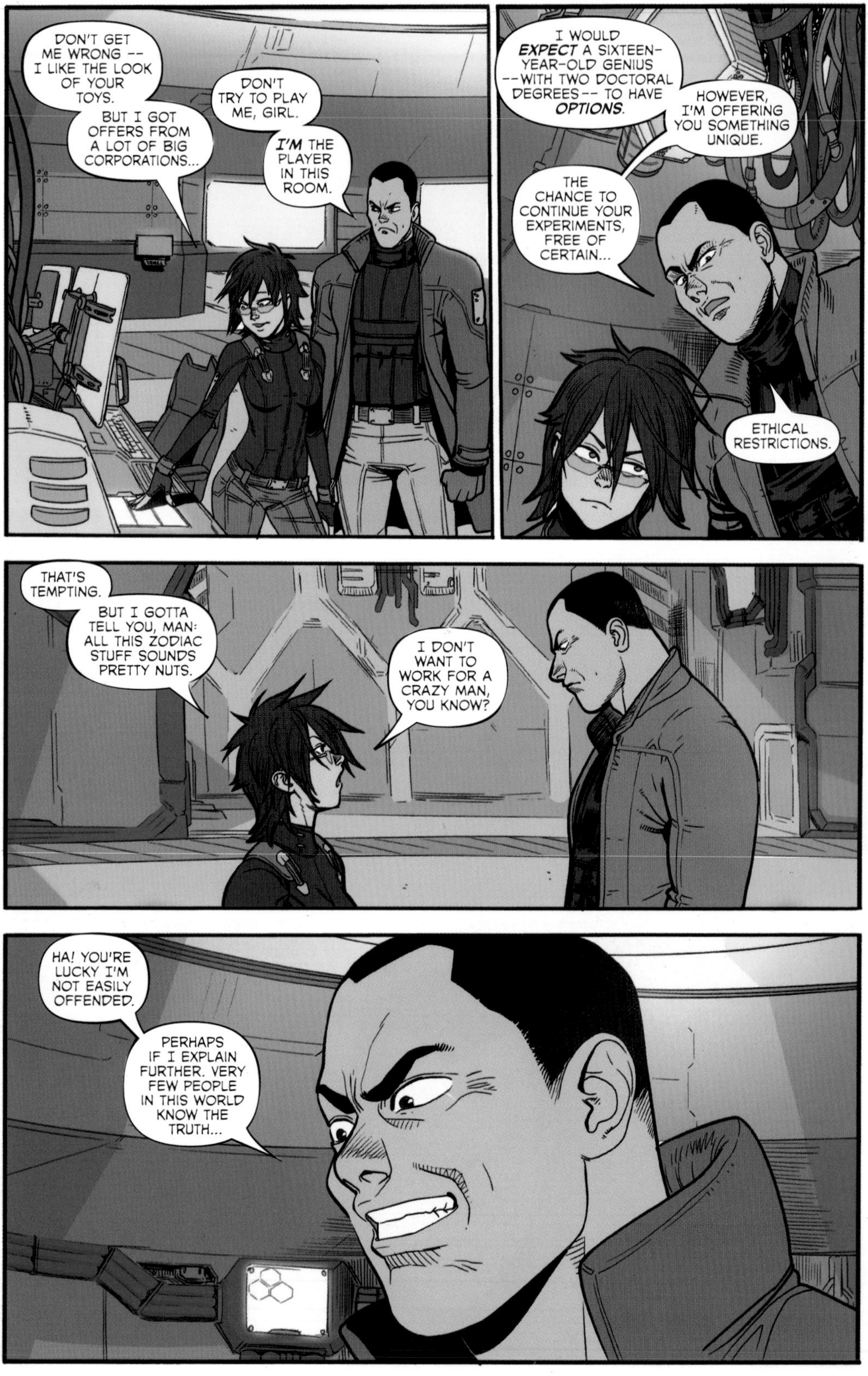
DON'T GET ME WRONG -- I LIKE THE LOOK OF YOUR TOYS.
BUT I GOT OFFERS FROM A LOT OF BIG CORPORATIONS...
DON'T TRY TO PLAY ME, GIRL.
I'M THE PLAYER IN THIS ROOM.
I WOULD EXPECT A SIXTEEN-YEAR-OLD GENIUS --WITH TWO DOCTORAL DEGREES-- TO HAVE OPTIONS.
HOWEVER, I'M OFFERING YOU SOMETHING UNIQUE.
THE CHANCE TO CONTINUE YOUR EXPERIMENTS, FREE OF CERTAIN...
ETHICAL RESTRICTIONS.
THAT'S TEMPTING.
BUT I GOTTA TELL YOU, MAN: ALL THIS ZODIAC STUFF SOUNDS PRETTY NUTS.
I DON'T WANT TO WORK FOR A CRAZY MAN, YOU KNOW?
HA! YOU'RE LUCKY I'M NOT EASILY OFFENDED.
PERHAPS IF I EXPLAIN FURTHER. VERY FEW PEOPLE IN THIS WORLD KNOW THE TRUTH...

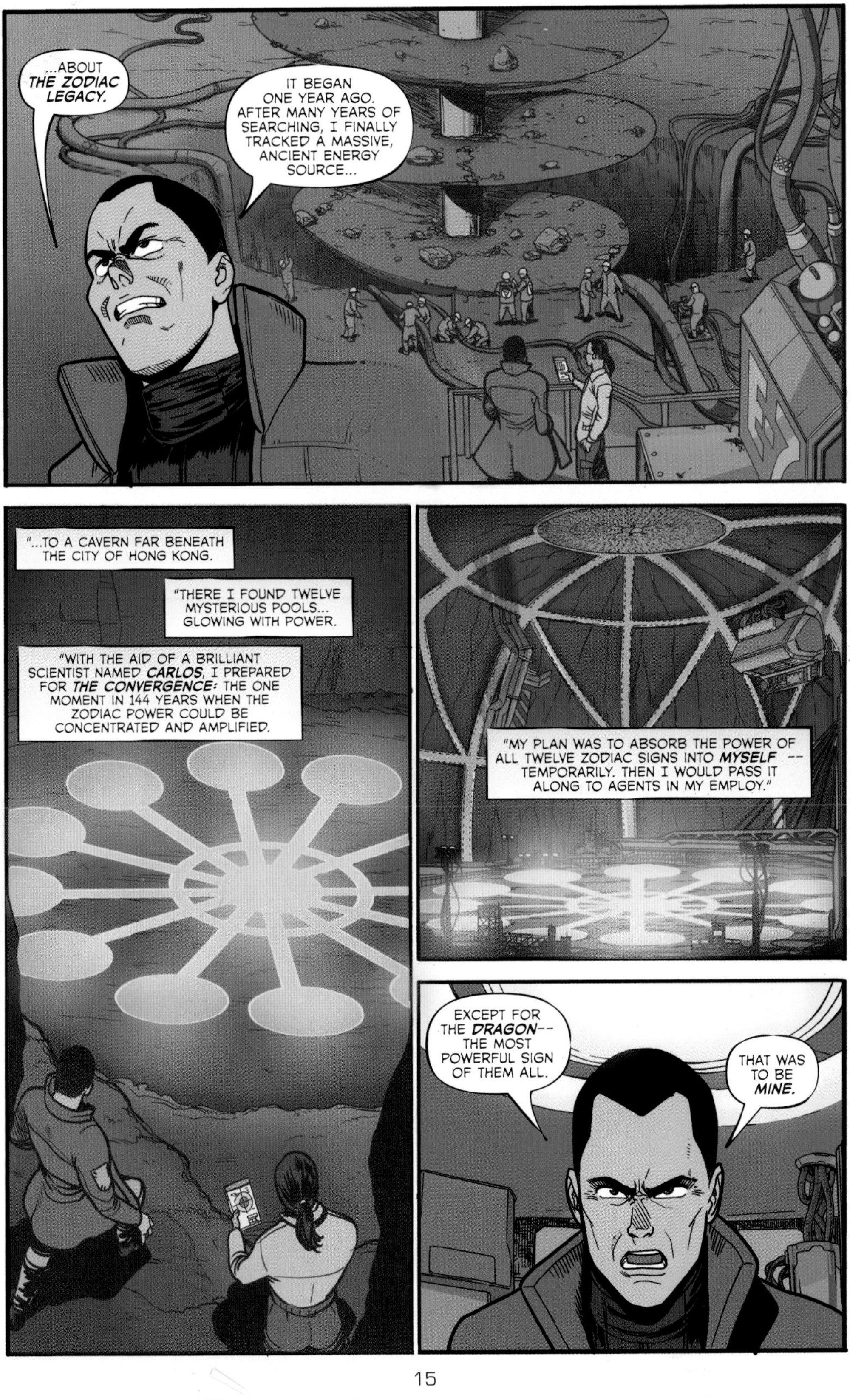

...ABOUT THE ZODIAC LEGACY.
IT BEGAN ONE YEAR AGO. AFTER MANY YEARS OF SEARCHING, I FINALLY TRACKED A MASSIVE, ANCIENT ENERGY SOURCE...
"...TO A CAVERN FAR BENEATH THE CITY OF HONG KONG.
"THERE I FOUND TWELVE MYSTERIOUS POOLS... GLOWING WITH POWER.
"WITH THE AID OF A BRILLIANT SCIENTIST NAMED CARLOS, I PREPARED FOR THE CONVERGENCE: THE ONE MOMENT IN 144 YEARS WHEN THE ZODIAC POWER COULD BE CONCENTRATED AND AMPLIFIED.
"MY PLAN WAS TO ABSORB THE POWER OF ALL TWELVE ZODIAC SIGNS INTO MYSELF -- TEMPORARILY. THEN I WOULD PASS IT ALONG TO AGENTS IN MY EMPLOY."
EXCEPT FOR THE DRAGON-- THE MOST POWERFUL SIGN OF THEM ALL.
THAT WAS TO BE MINE.

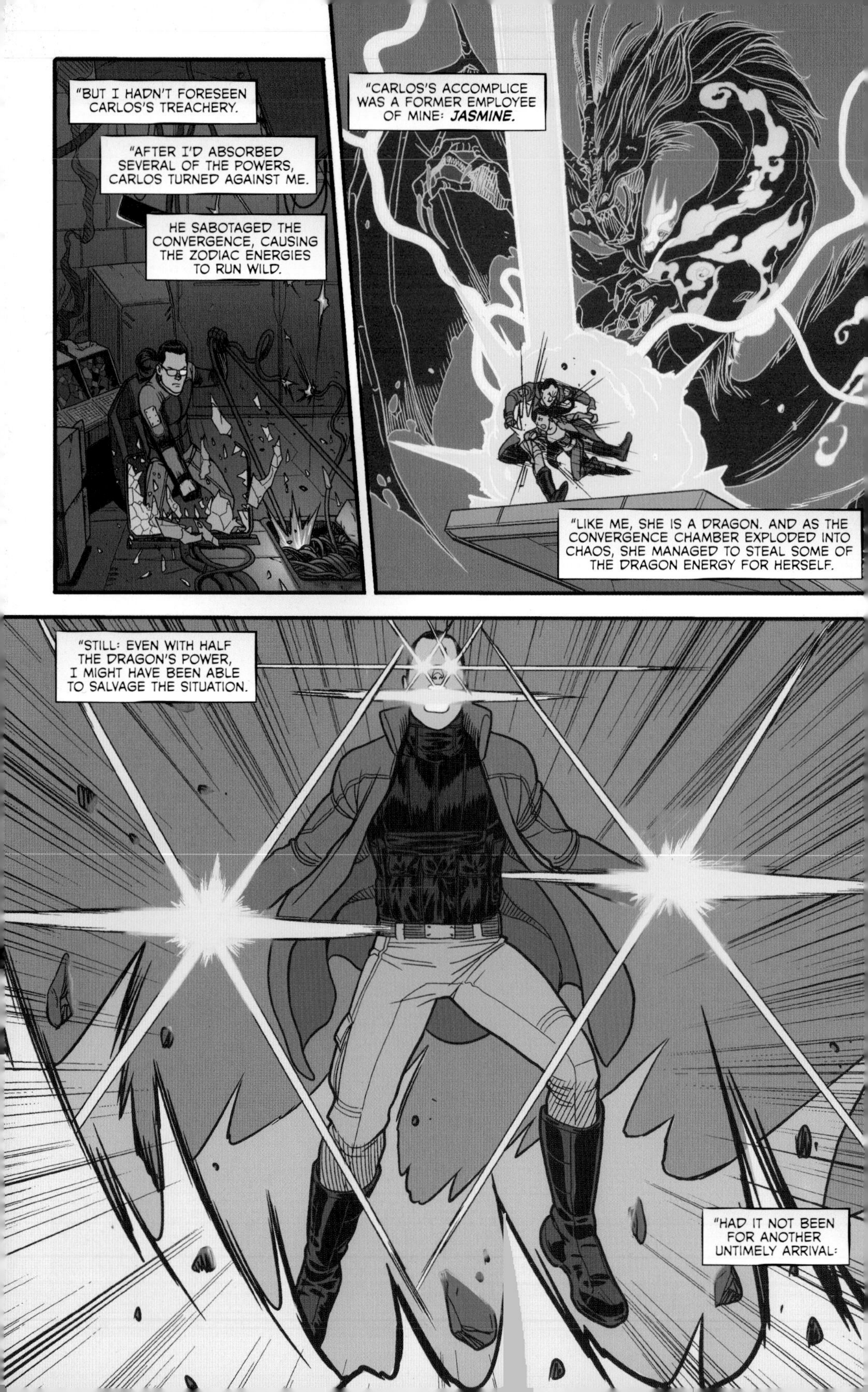
"BUT I HADN'T FORESEEN CARLOS'S TREACHERY.
"AFTER I'D ABSORBED SEVERAL OF THE POWERS, CARLOS TURNED AGAINST ME.
HE SABOTAGED THE CONVERGENCE, CAUSING THE ZODIAC ENERGIES TO RUN WILD.
"CARLOS'S ACCOMPLICE WAS A FORMER EMPLOYEE OF MINE: JASMINE.
"LIKE ME, SHE IS A DRAGON. AND AS THE CONVERGENCE CHAMBER EXPLODED INTO CHAOS, SHE MANAGED TO STEAL SOME OF THE DRAGON ENERGY FOR HERSELF.
"STILL: EVEN WITH HALF THE DRAGON'S POWER, I MIGHT HAVE BEEN ABLE TO SALVAGE THE SITUATION.
"HAD IT NOT BEEN FOR ANOTHER UNTIMELY ARRIVAL:

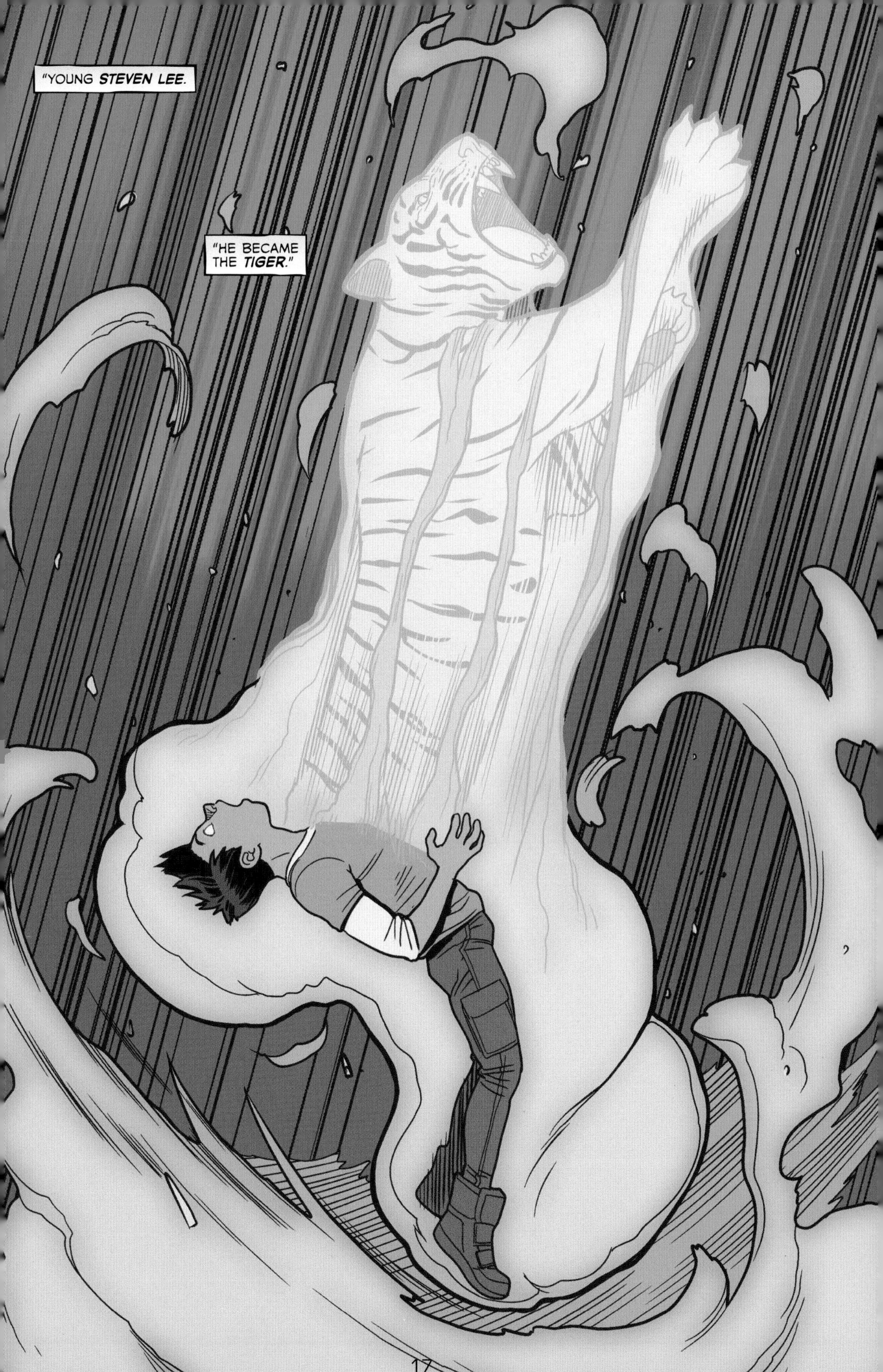
"YOUNG STEVEN LEE.
"HE BECAME THE TIGER."

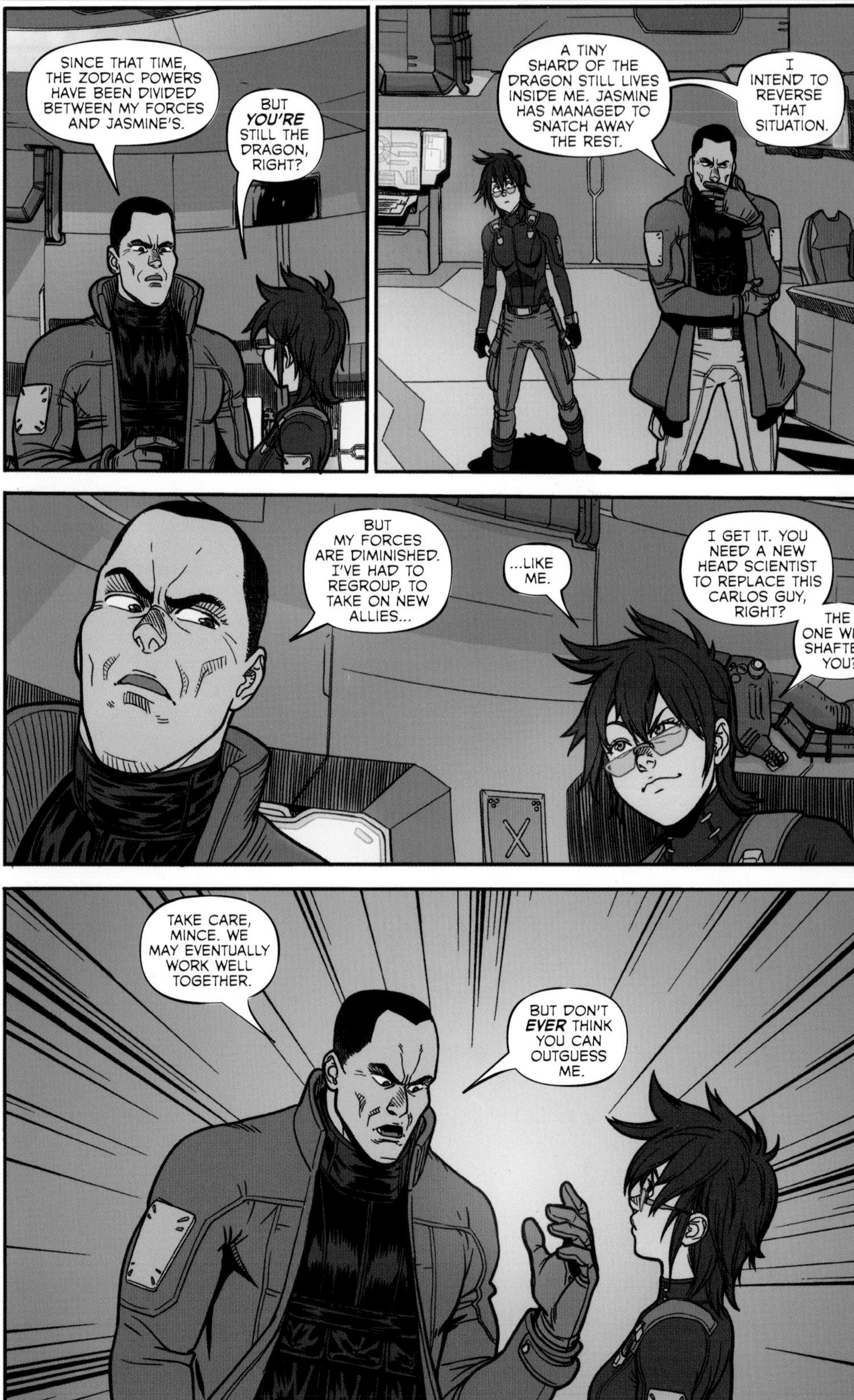
SINCE THAT TIME, THE ZODIAC POWERS HAVE BEEN DIVIDED BETWEEN MY FORCES AND JASMINE'S.
BUT *YOU'RE* STILL THE DRAGON, RIGHT?
A TINY SHARD OF THE DRAGON STILL LIVES INSIDE ME. JASMINE HAS MANAGED TO SNATCH AWAY THE REST.
I INTEND TO REVERSE THAT SITUATION.
BUT MY FORCES ARE DIMINISHED. I'VE HAD TO REGROUP, TO TAKE ON NEW ALLIES...
...LIKE ME.
I GET IT. YOU NEED A NEW HEAD SCIENTIST TO REPLACE THIS CARLOS GUY, RIGHT?
THE ONE WHO SHAFTED YOU?
TAKE CARE, MINCE. WE MAY EVENTUALLY WORK WELL TOGETHER.
BUT DON'T *EVER* THINK YOU CAN OUTGUESS ME.

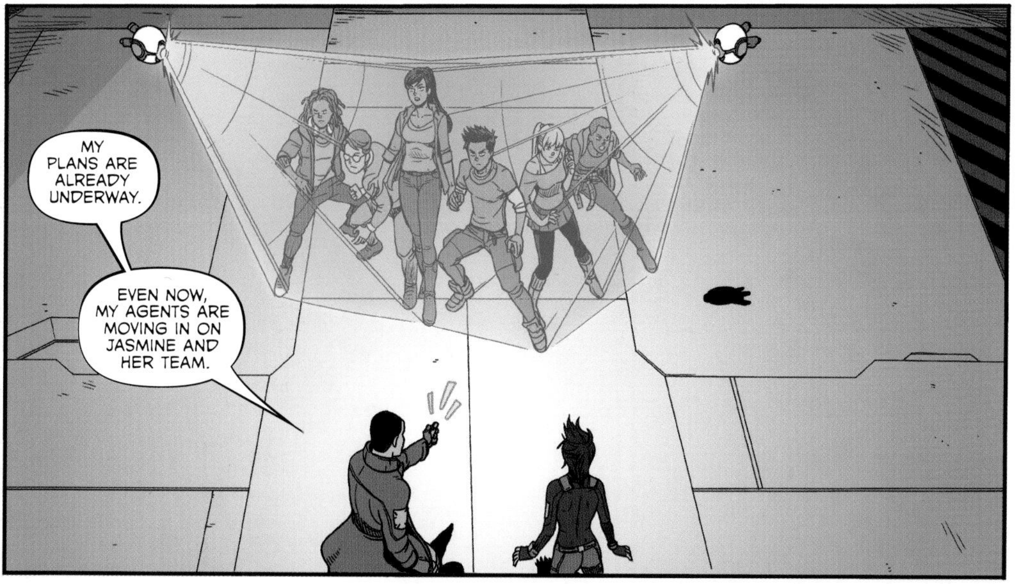
MY PLANS ARE ALREADY UNDERWAY.
EVEN NOW, MY AGENTS ARE MOVING IN ON JASMINE AND HER TEAM.

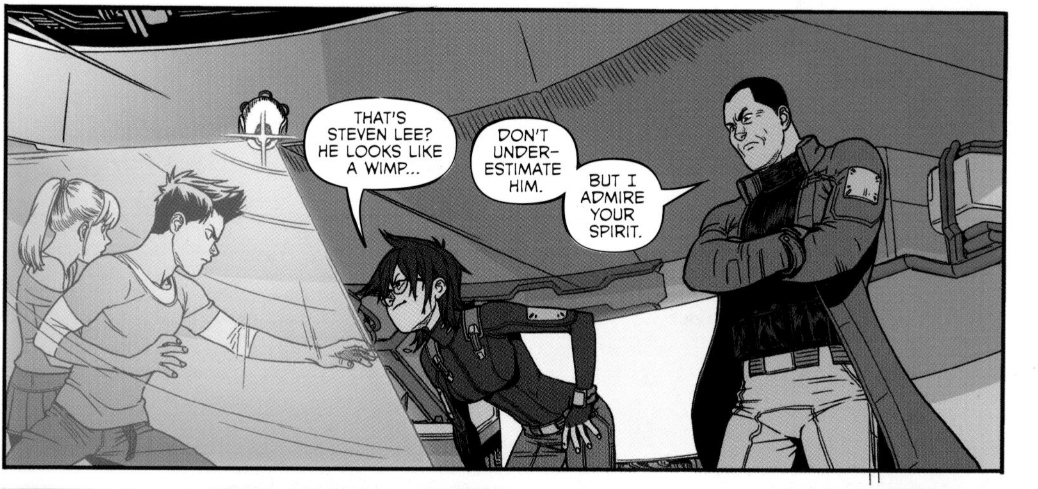
THAT'S STEVEN LEE? HE LOOKS LIKE A WIMP...
DON'T UNDER-ESTIMATE HIM.
BUT I ADMIRE YOUR SPIRIT.

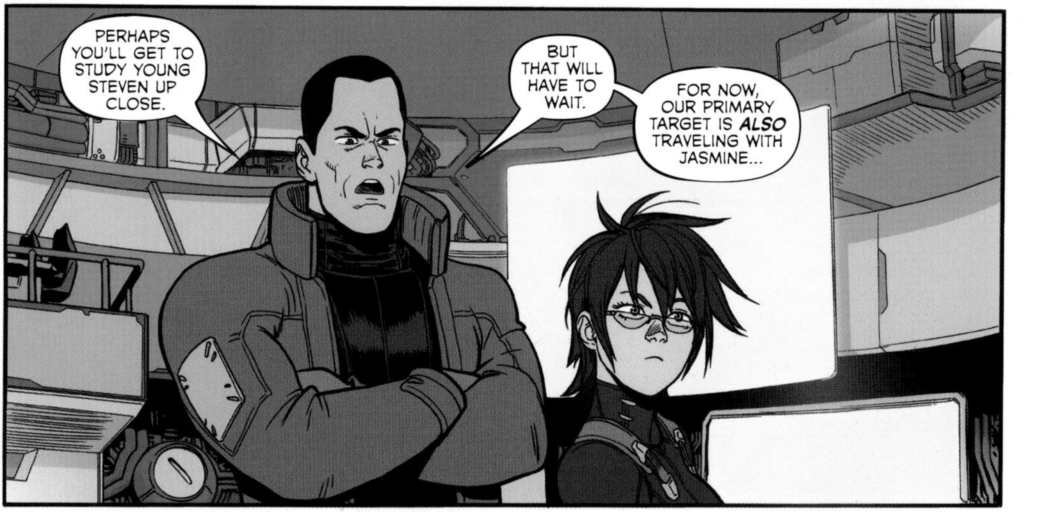
PERHAPS YOU'LL GET TO STUDY YOUNG STEVEN UP CLOSE.
BUT THAT WILL HAVE TO WAIT.
FOR NOW, OUR PRIMARY TARGET IS ***ALSO*** TRAVELING WITH JASMINE...

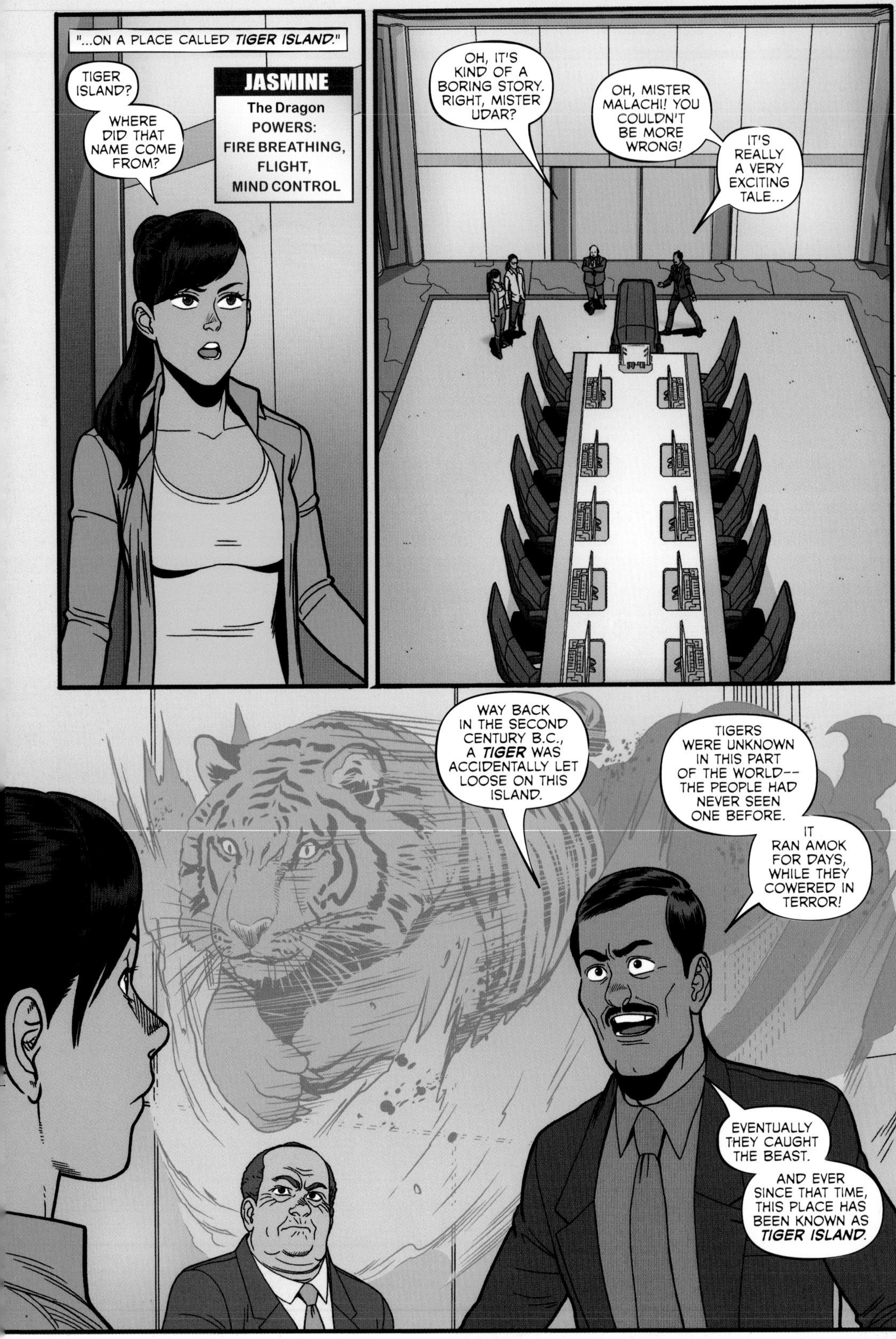
"...ON A PLACE CALLED TIGER ISLAND."
TIGER ISLAND?
WHERE DID THAT NAME COME FROM?
JASMINE
The Dragon
POWERS:
FIRE BREATHING,
FLIGHT,
MIND CONTROL
OH, IT'S KIND OF A BORING STORY. RIGHT, MISTER UDAR?
OH, MISTER MALACHI! YOU COULDN'T BE MORE WRONG!
IT'S REALLY A VERY EXCITING TALE...
WAY BACK IN THE SECOND CENTURY B.C., A TIGER WAS ACCIDENTALLY LET LOOSE ON THIS ISLAND.
TIGERS WERE UNKNOWN IN THIS PART OF THE WORLD-- THE PEOPLE HAD NEVER SEEN ONE BEFORE.
IT RAN AMOK FOR DAYS, WHILE THEY COWERED IN TERROR!
EVENTUALLY THEY CAUGHT THE BEAST.
AND EVER SINCE THAT TIME, THIS PLACE HAS BEEN KNOWN AS TIGER ISLAND.

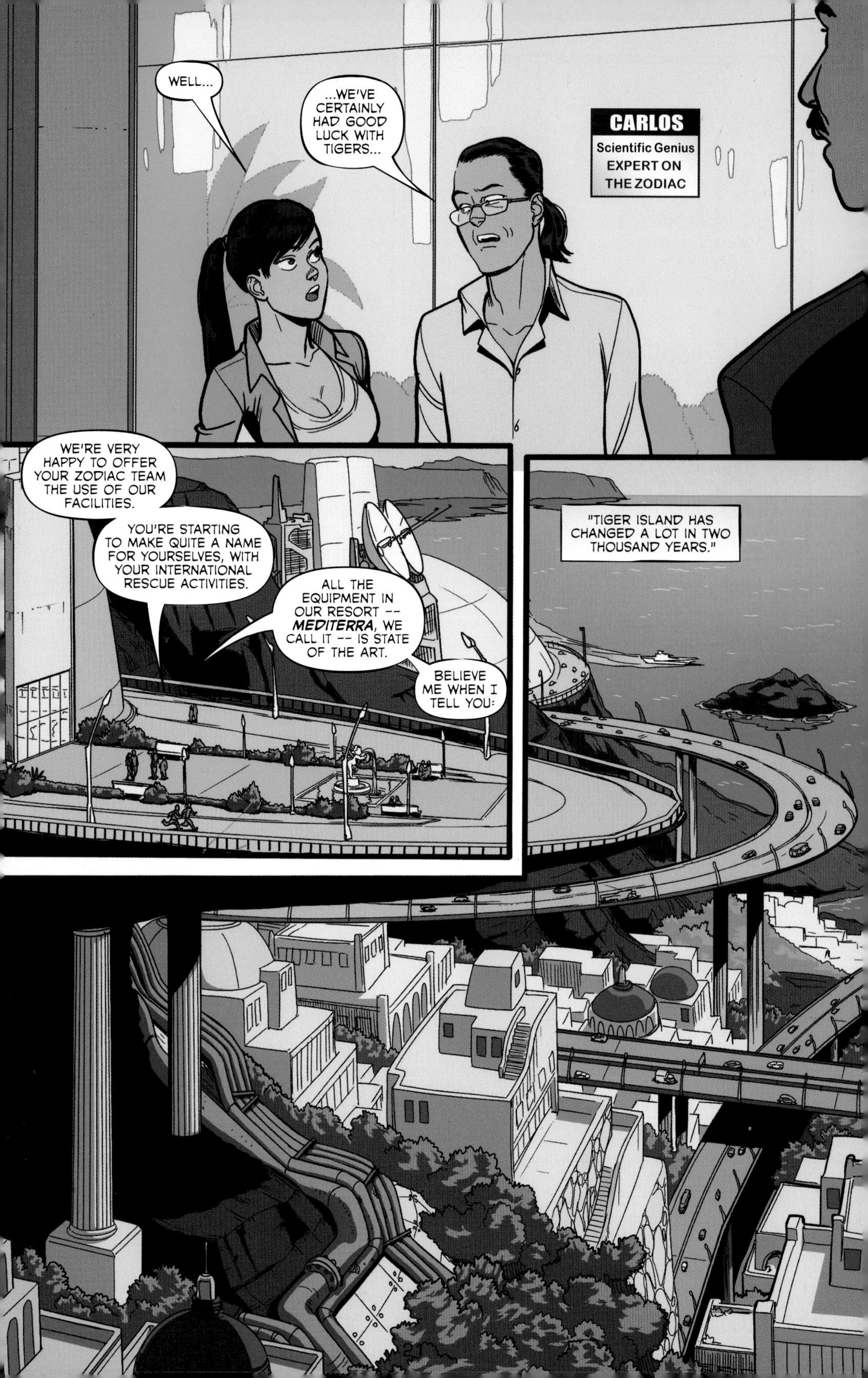
WELL...
...WE'VE CERTAINLY HAD GOOD LUCK WITH TIGERS...
CARLOS
Scientific Genius
EXPERT ON THE ZODIAC
WE'RE VERY HAPPY TO OFFER YOUR ZODIAC TEAM THE USE OF OUR FACILITIES.
YOU'RE STARTING TO MAKE QUITE A NAME FOR YOURSELVES, WITH YOUR INTERNATIONAL RESCUE ACTIVITIES.
ALL THE EQUIPMENT IN OUR RESORT -- *MEDITERRA*, WE CALL IT -- IS STATE OF THE ART.
BELIEVE ME WHEN I TELL YOU:
"TIGER ISLAND HAS CHANGED A LOT IN TWO THOUSAND YEARS."

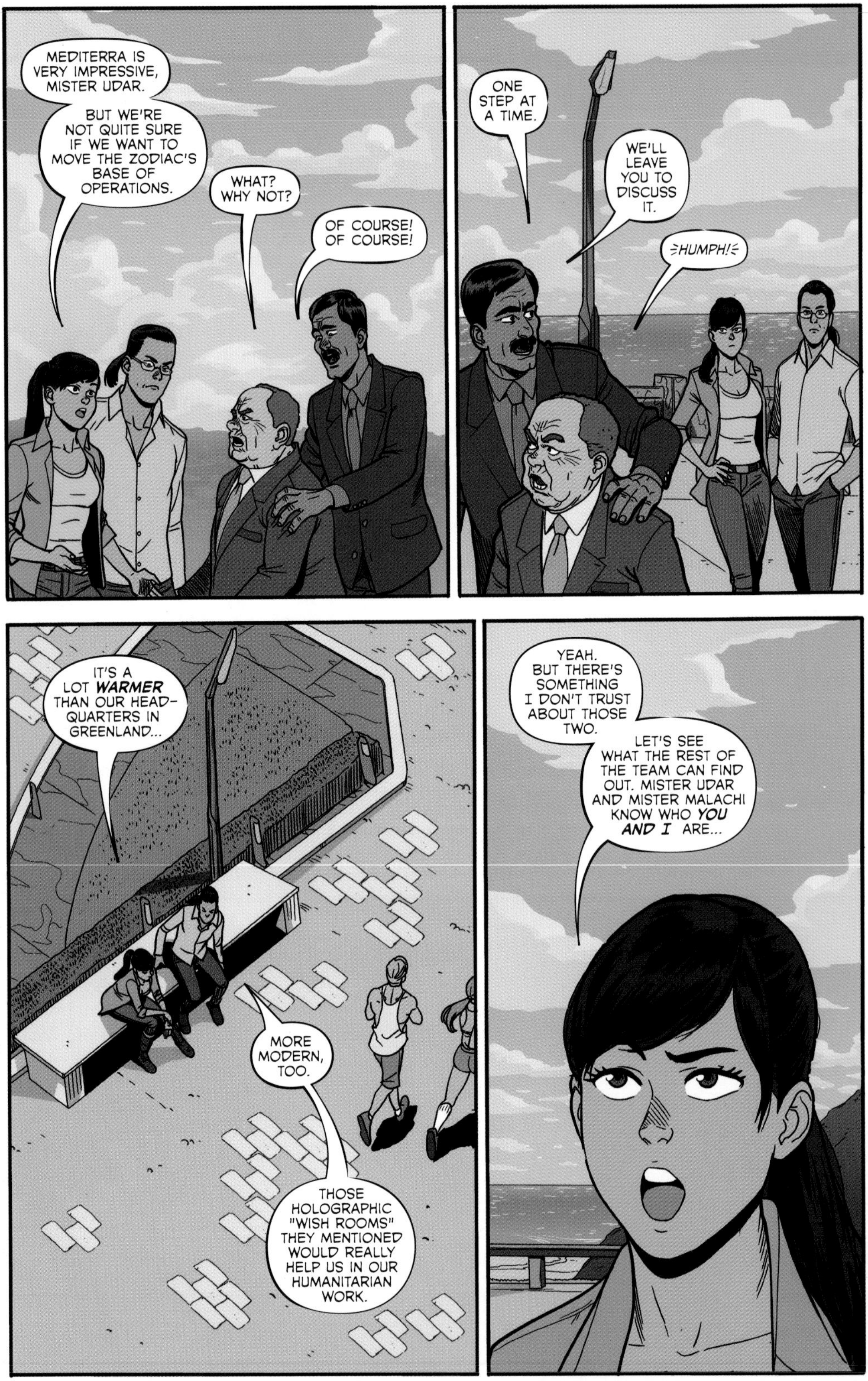
MEDITERRA IS VERY IMPRESSIVE, MISTER UDAR.
BUT WE'RE NOT QUITE SURE IF WE WANT TO MOVE THE ZODIAC'S BASE OF OPERATIONS.
WHAT? WHY NOT?
OF COURSE! OF COURSE!
ONE STEP AT A TIME.
WE'LL LEAVE YOU TO DISCUSS IT.
HUMPH!
IT'S A LOT **WARMER** THAN OUR HEAD-QUARTERS IN GREENLAND...
MORE MODERN, TOO.
THOSE HOLOGRAPHIC "WISH ROOMS" THEY MENTIONED WOULD REALLY HELP US IN OUR HUMANITARIAN WORK.
YEAH. BUT THERE'S SOMETHING I DON'T TRUST ABOUT THOSE TWO.
LET'S SEE WHAT THE REST OF THE TEAM CAN FIND OUT. MISTER UDAR AND MISTER MALACHI KNOW WHO ***YOU AND I*** ARE...

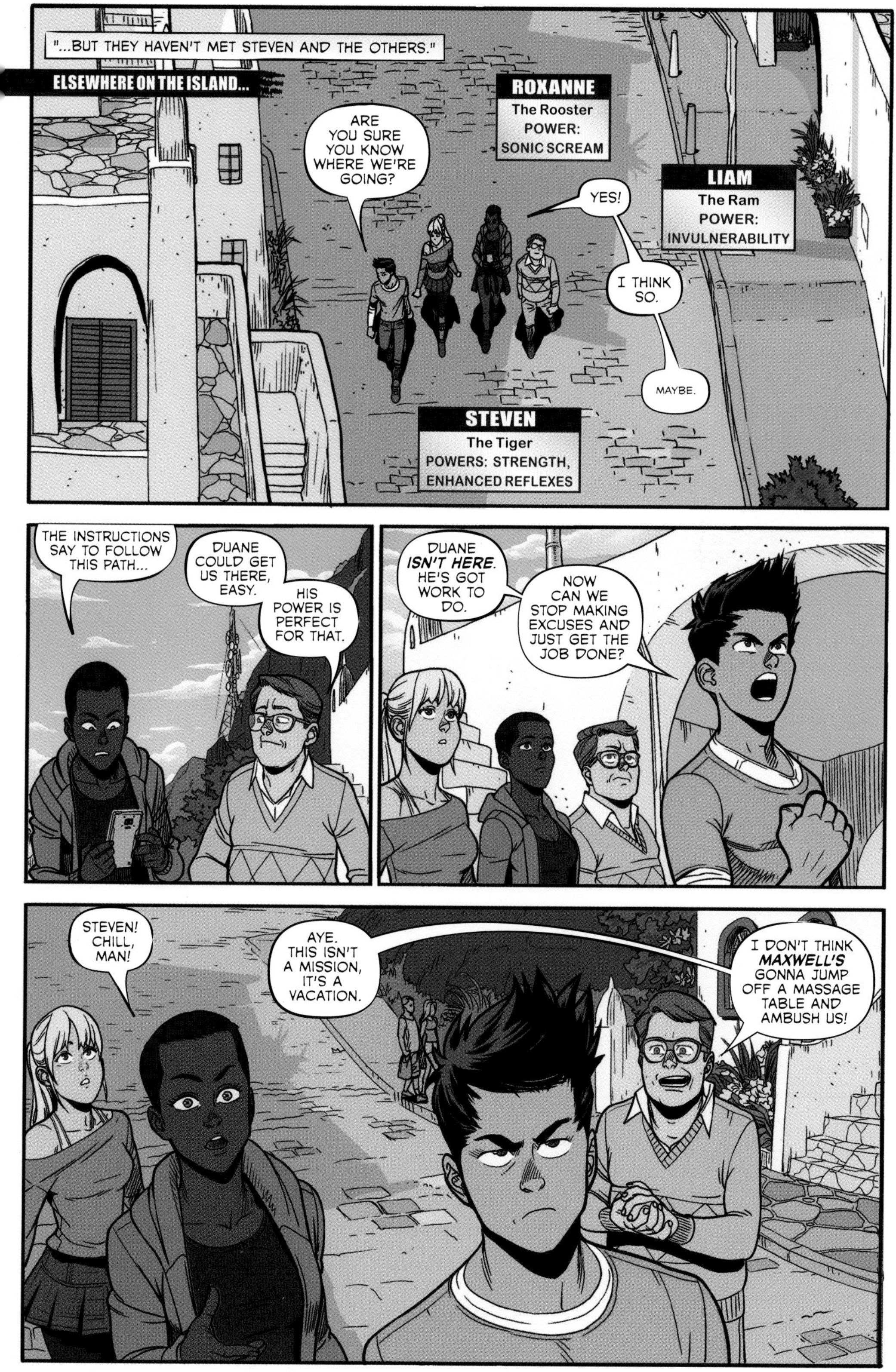
"...BUT THEY HAVEN'T MET STEVEN AND THE OTHERS."
ELSEWHERE ON THE ISLAND...
ROXANNE
The Rooster
POWER:
SONIC SCREAM
ARE YOU SURE YOU KNOW WHERE WE'RE GOING?
LIAM
The Ram
POWER:
INVULNERABILITY
YES!
I THINK SO.
MAYBE.
STEVEN
The Tiger
POWERS: STRENGTH,
ENHANCED REFLEXES
THE INSTRUCTIONS SAY TO FOLLOW THIS PATH...
DUANE COULD GET US THERE, EASY.
HIS POWER IS PERFECT FOR THAT.
DUANE ISN'T HERE. HE'S GOT WORK TO DO.
NOW CAN WE STOP MAKING EXCUSES AND JUST GET THE JOB DONE?
STEVEN! CHILL, MAN!
AYE. THIS ISN'T A MISSION, IT'S A VACATION.
I DON'T THINK MAXWELL'S GONNA JUMP OFF A MASSAGE TABLE AND AMBUSH US!

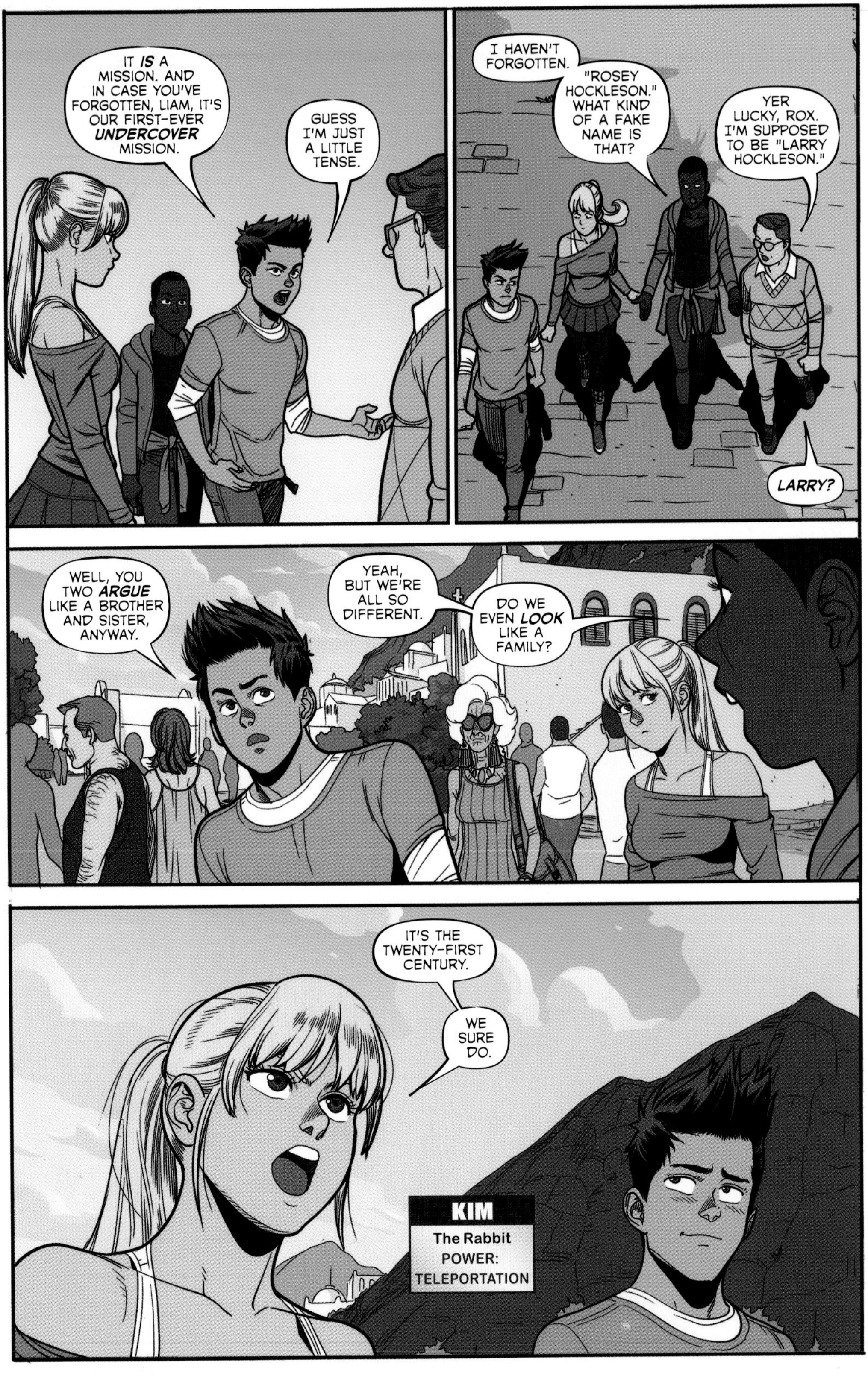
IT IS A MISSION. AND IN CASE YOU'VE FORGOTTEN, LIAM, IT'S OUR FIRST-EVER UNDERCOVER MISSION.
GUESS I'M JUST A LITTLE TENSE.
I HAVEN'T FORGOTTEN.
"ROSEY HOCKLESON." WHAT KIND OF A FAKE NAME IS THAT?
YER LUCKY, ROX. I'M SUPPOSED TO BE "LARRY HOCKLESON."
LARRY?
WELL, YOU TWO ARGUE LIKE A BROTHER AND SISTER, ANYWAY.
YEAH, BUT WE'RE ALL SO DIFFERENT.
DO WE EVEN LOOK LIKE A FAMILY?
IT'S THE TWENTY-FIRST CENTURY.
WE SURE DO.
KIM
The Rabbit
POWER:
TELEPORTATION

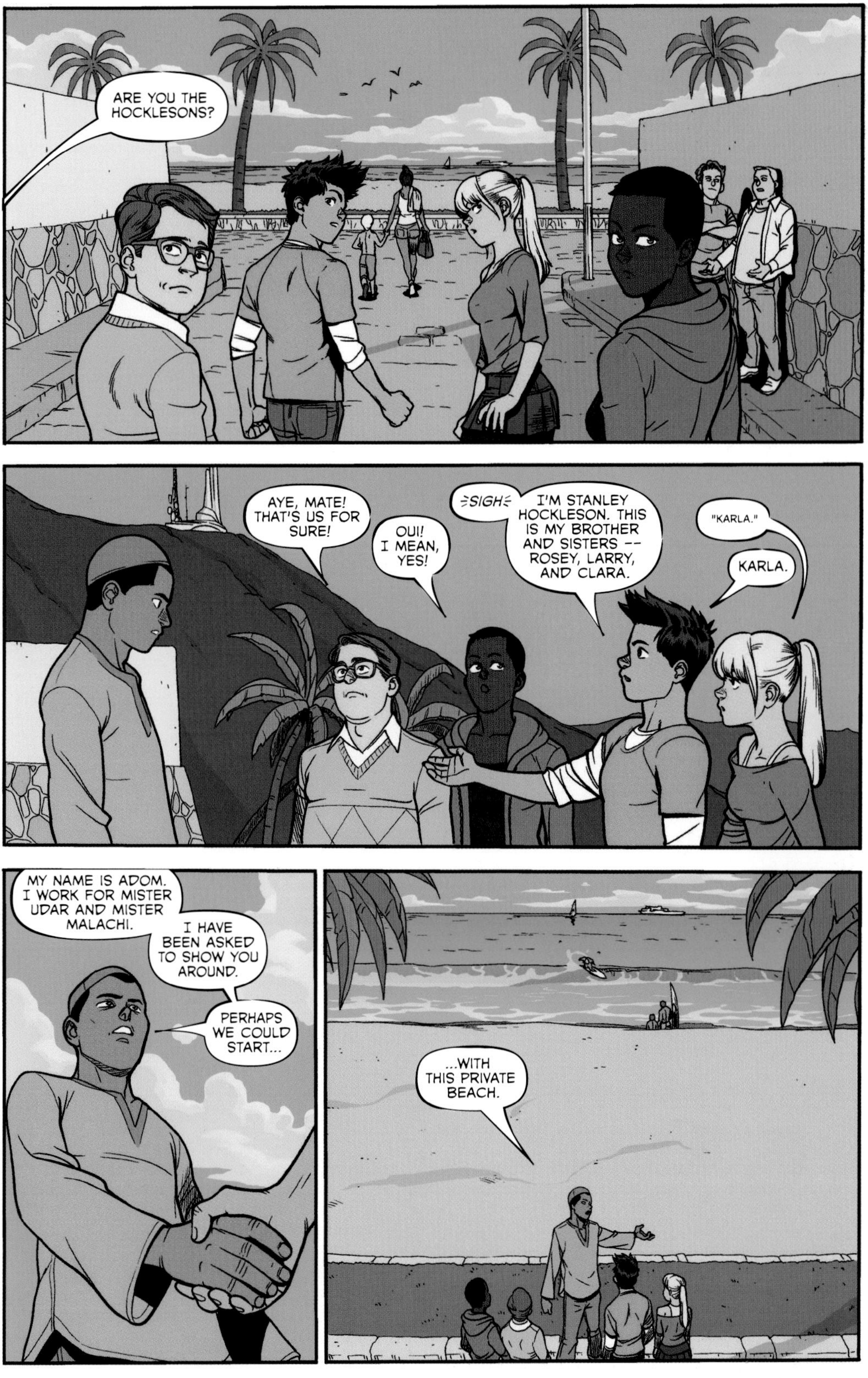

ARE YOU THE HOCKLESONS?
AYE, MATE! THAT'S US FOR SURE!
OUI! I MEAN, YES!
SIGH
I'M STANLEY HOCKLESON. THIS IS MY BROTHER AND SISTERS -- ROSEY, LARRY, AND CLARA.
"KARLA."
KARLA.
MY NAME IS ADOM. I WORK FOR MISTER UDAR AND MISTER MALACHI.
I HAVE BEEN ASKED TO SHOW YOU AROUND.
PERHAPS WE COULD START...
...WITH THIS PRIVATE BEACH.

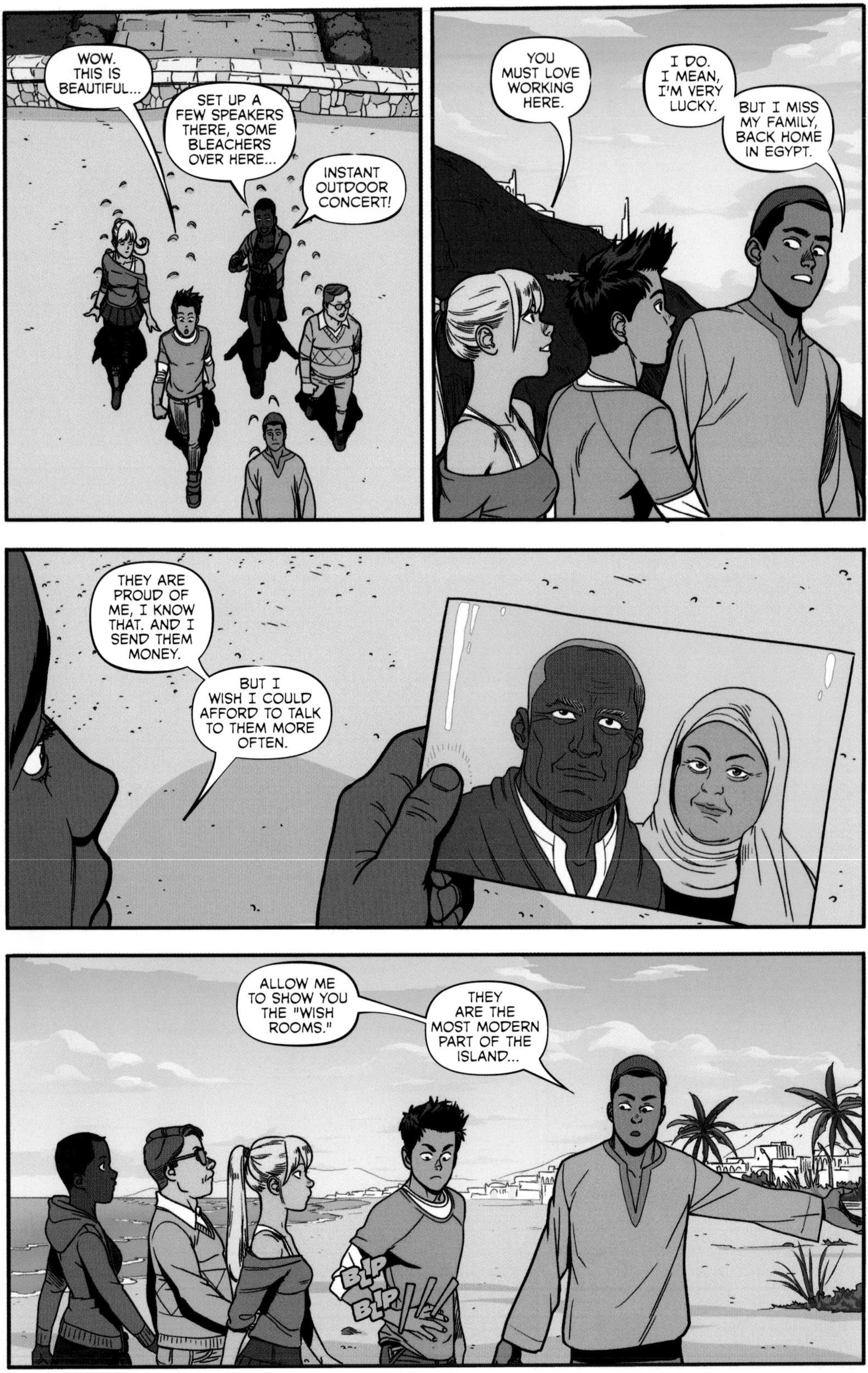
WOW. THIS IS BEAUTIFUL...
SET UP A FEW SPEAKERS THERE, SOME BLEACHERS OVER HERE...
INSTANT OUTDOOR CONCERT!
YOU MUST LOVE WORKING HERE.
I DO. I MEAN, I'M VERY LUCKY.
BUT I MISS MY FAMILY, BACK HOME IN EGYPT.
THEY ARE PROUD OF ME, I KNOW THAT. AND I SEND THEM MONEY.
BUT I WISH I COULD AFFORD TO TALK TO THEM MORE OFTEN.
ALLOW ME TO SHOW YOU THE "WISH ROOMS."
THEY ARE THE MOST MODERN PART OF THE ISLAND...
BLIP BLIP

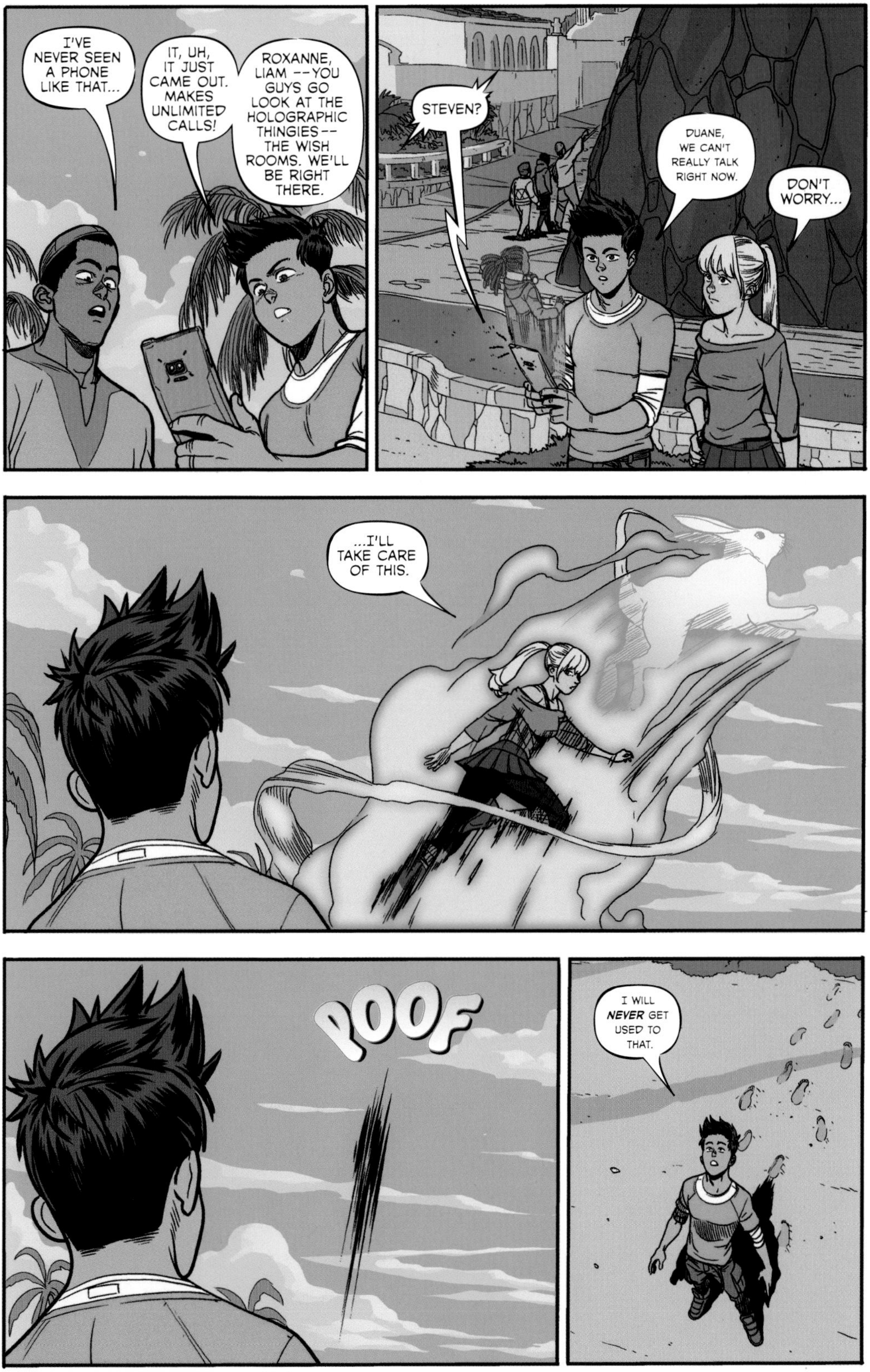
I'VE NEVER SEEN A PHONE LIKE THAT...
IT, UH, IT JUST CAME OUT. MAKES UNLIMITED CALLS!
ROXANNE, LIAM --YOU GUYS GO LOOK AT THE HOLOGRAPHIC THINGIES-- THE WISH ROOMS. WE'LL BE RIGHT THERE.
STEVEN?
DUANE, WE CAN'T REALLY TALK RIGHT NOW.
DON'T WORRY...
...I'LL TAKE CARE OF THIS.
POOF
I WILL ***NEVER*** GET USED TO THAT.

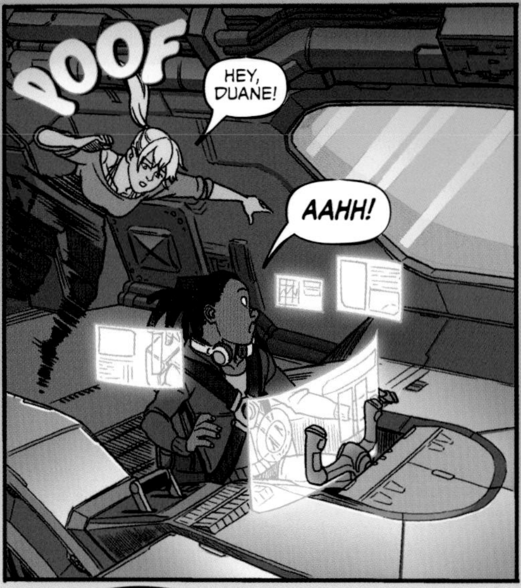
POOF
HEY, DUANE!
AAHH!

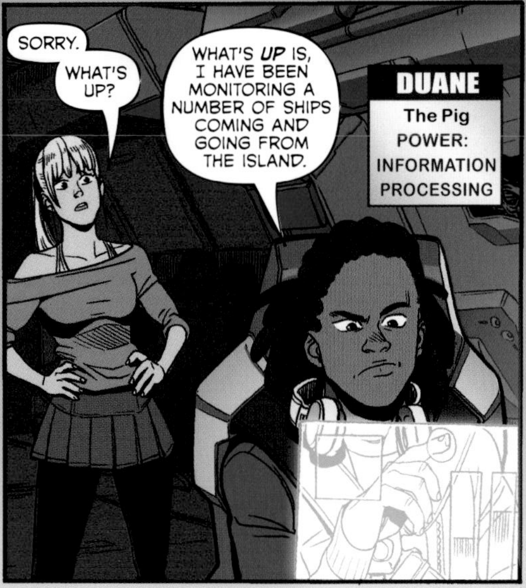
SORRY.
WHAT'S UP?
WHAT'S UP IS, I HAVE BEEN MONITORING A NUMBER OF SHIPS COMING AND GOING FROM THE ISLAND.
DUANE
The Pig
POWER: INFORMATION PROCESSING

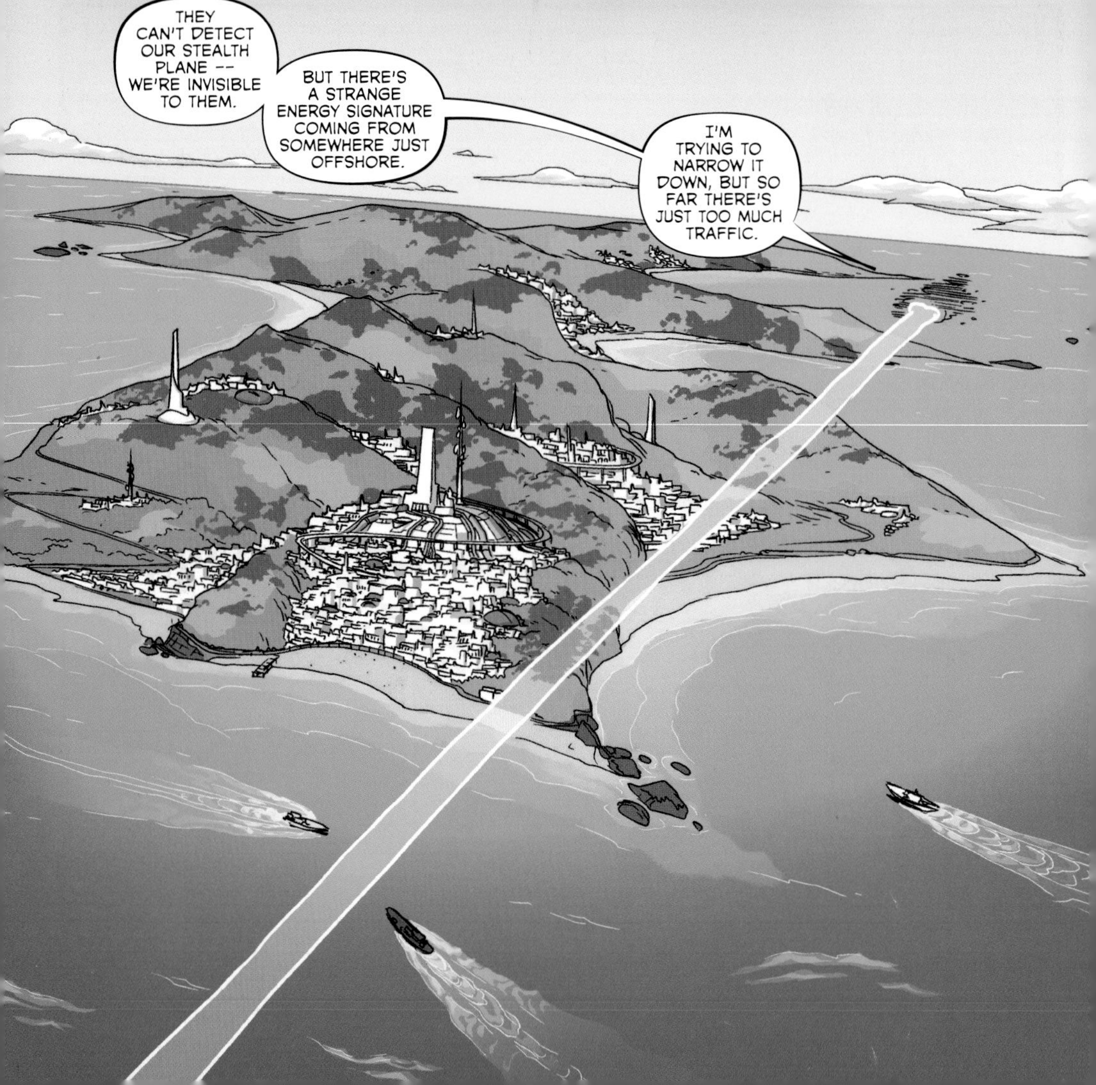
THEY CAN'T DETECT OUR STEALTH PLANE -- WE'RE INVISIBLE TO THEM.
BUT THERE'S A STRANGE ENERGY SIGNATURE COMING FROM SOMEWHERE JUST OFFSHORE.
I'M TRYING TO NARROW IT DOWN, BUT SO FAR THERE'S JUST TOO MUCH TRAFFIC.

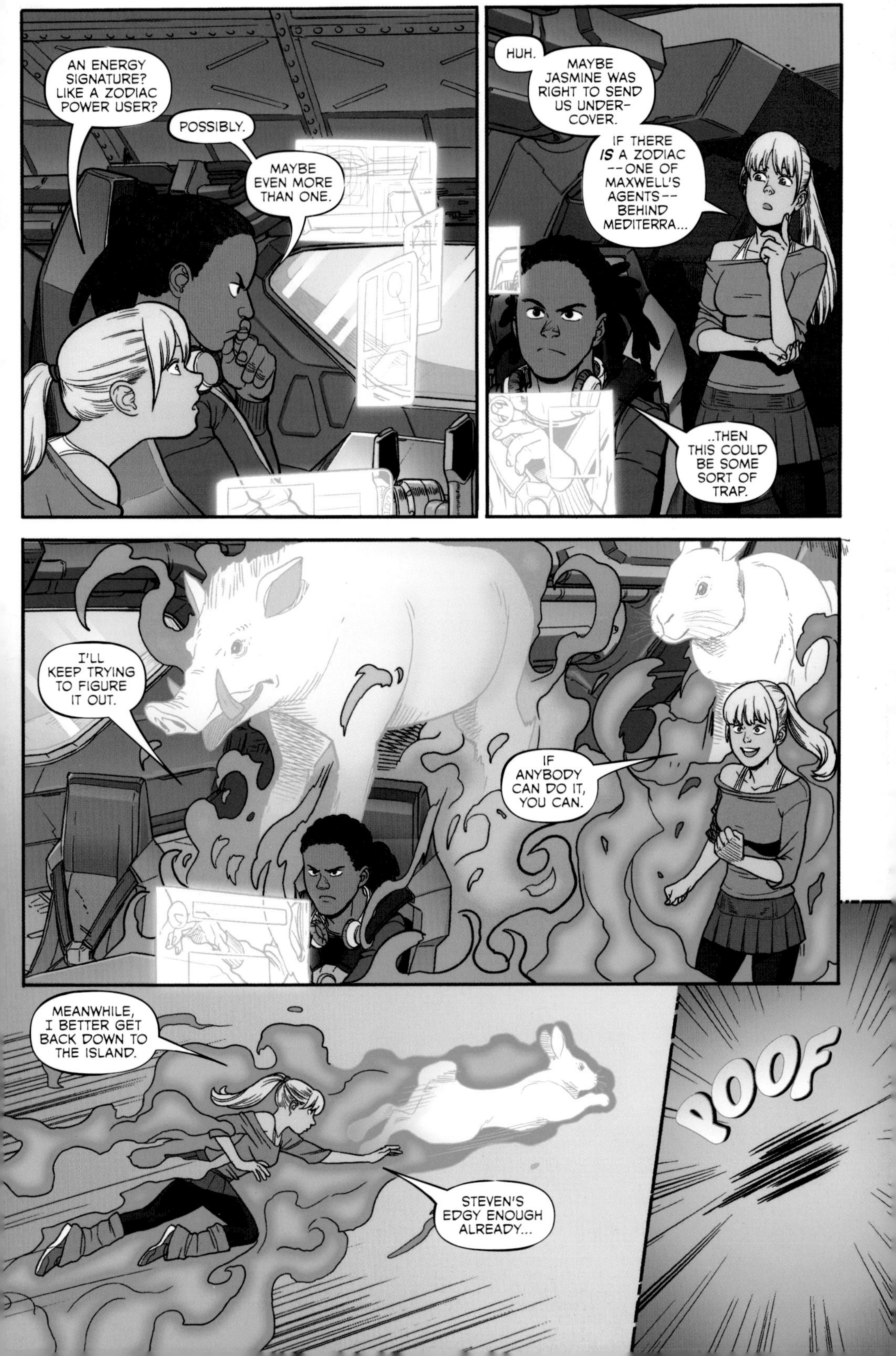
AN ENERGY SIGNATURE? LIKE A ZODIAC POWER USER?
POSSIBLY.
MAYBE EVEN MORE THAN ONE.
HUH.
MAYBE JASMINE WAS RIGHT TO SEND US UNDER-COVER.
IF THERE IS A ZODIAC --ONE OF MAXWELL'S AGENTS-- BEHIND MEDITERRA...
..THEN THIS COULD BE SOME SORT OF TRAP.
I'LL KEEP TRYING TO FIGURE IT OUT.
IF ANYBODY CAN DO IT, YOU CAN.
MEANWHILE, I BETTER GET BACK DOWN TO THE ISLAND.
STEVEN'S EDGY ENOUGH ALREADY...
POOF

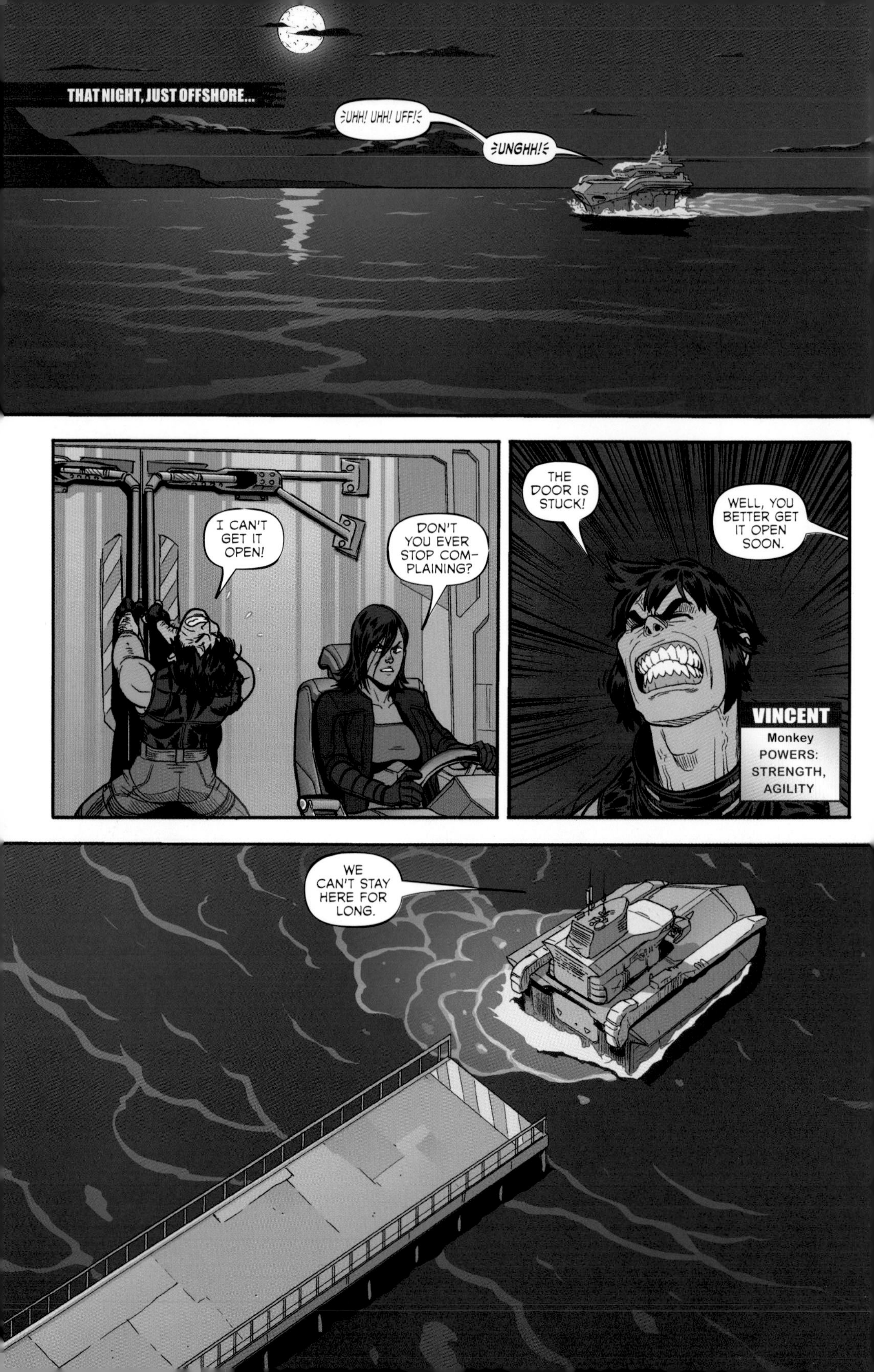
THAT NIGHT, JUST OFFSHORE...
UHH! UHH! UFF!
UNGHH!
I CAN'T GET IT OPEN!
DON'T YOU EVER STOP COMPLAINING?
THE DOOR IS STUCK!
WELL, YOU BETTER GET IT OPEN SOON.
VINCENT
Monkey
POWERS: STRENGTH, AGILITY
WE CAN'T STAY HERE FOR LONG.

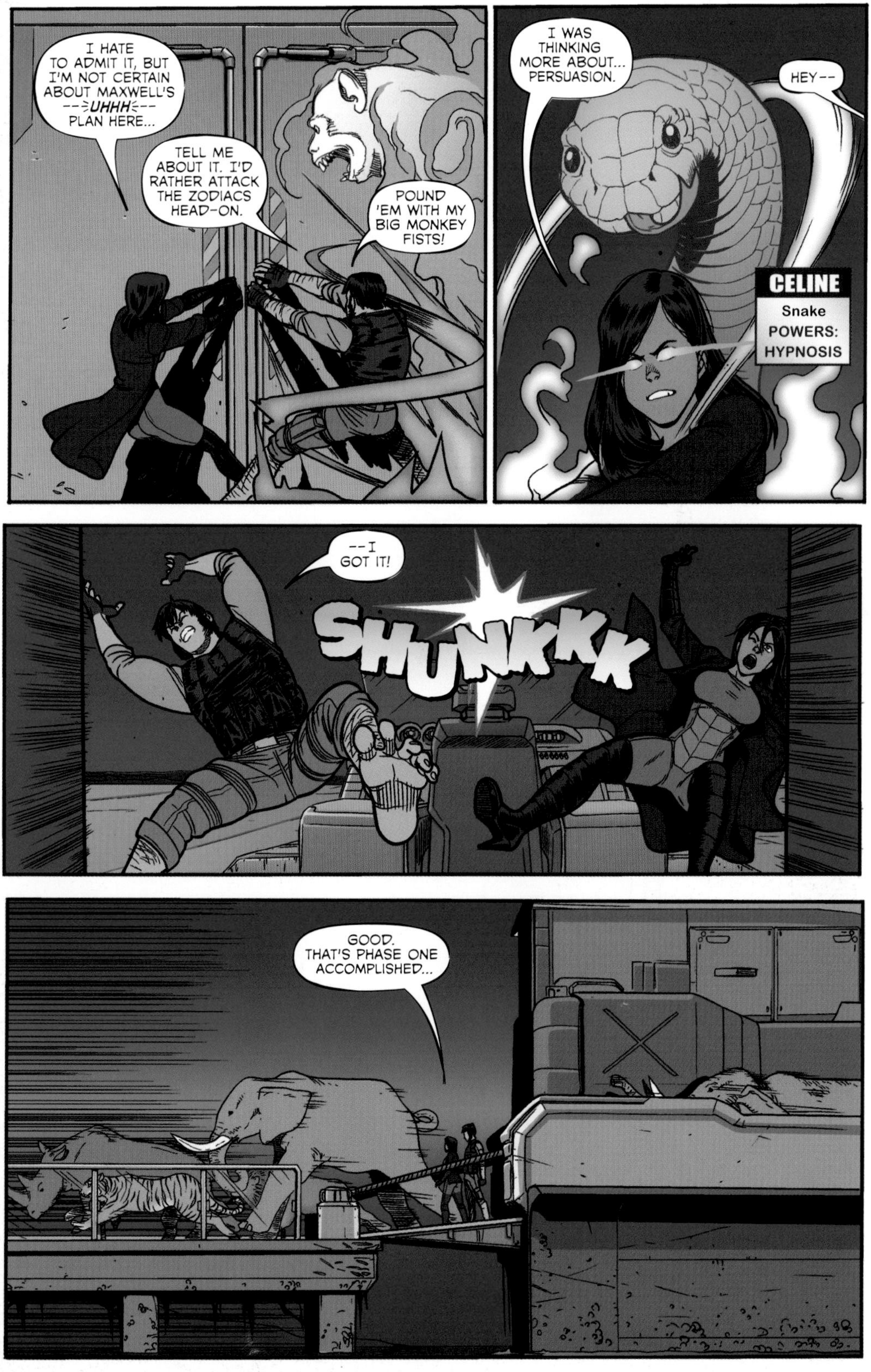
I HATE TO ADMIT IT, BUT I'M NOT CERTAIN ABOUT MAXWELL'S --UHHH-- PLAN HERE...
TELL ME ABOUT IT. I'D RATHER ATTACK THE ZODIACS HEAD-ON.
POUND 'EM WITH MY BIG MONKEY FISTS!
I WAS THINKING MORE ABOUT... PERSUASION.
HEY--
CELINE
Snake
POWERS: HYPNOSIS
--I GOT IT!
SHUNKKK
GOOD. THAT'S PHASE ONE ACCOMPLISHED...

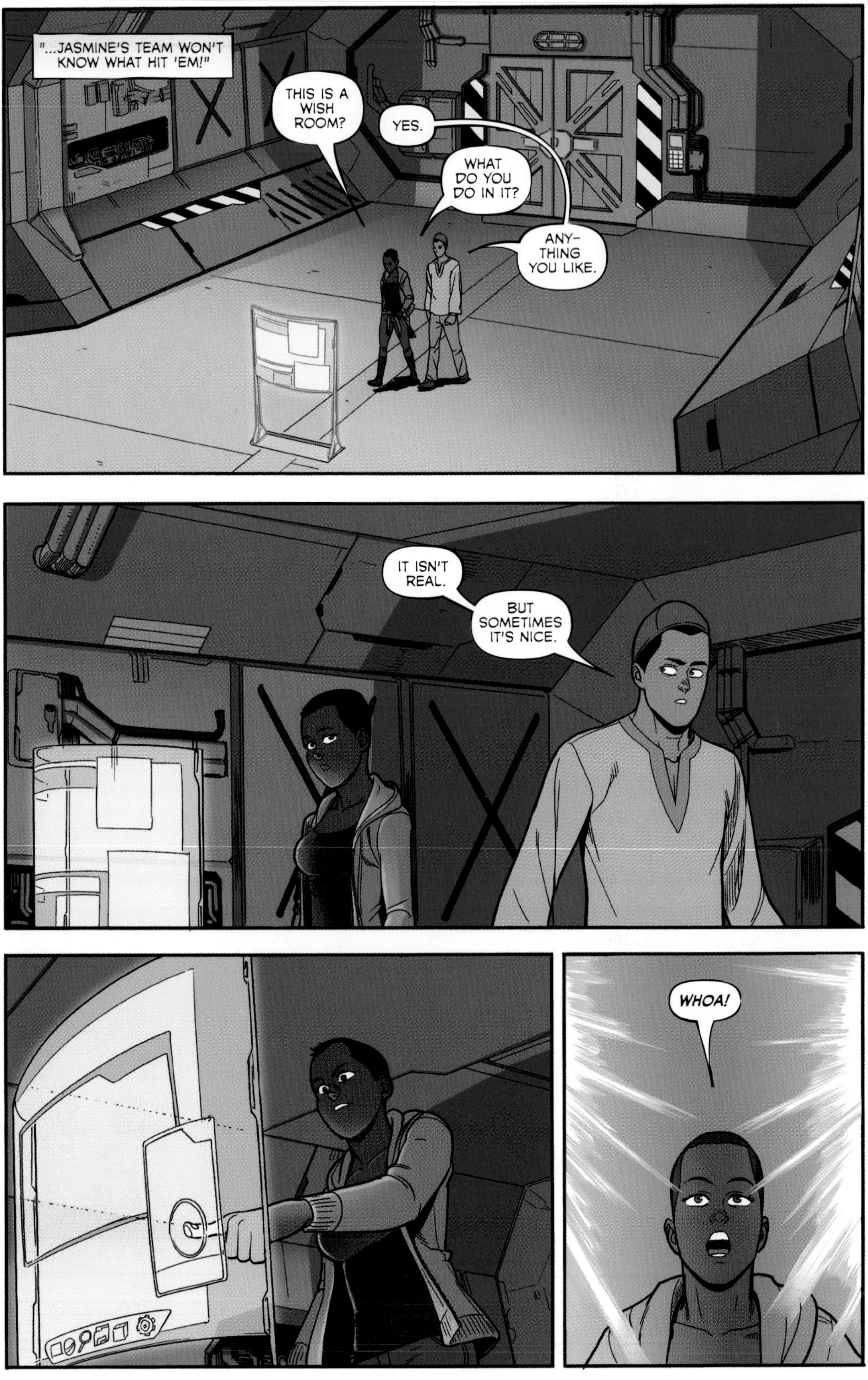
"...JASMINE'S TEAM WON'T KNOW WHAT HIT 'EM!"
THIS IS A WISH ROOM?
YES.
WHAT DO YOU DO IN IT?
ANY-THING YOU LIKE.
IT ISN'T REAL.
BUT SOMETIMES IT'S NICE.
WHOA!

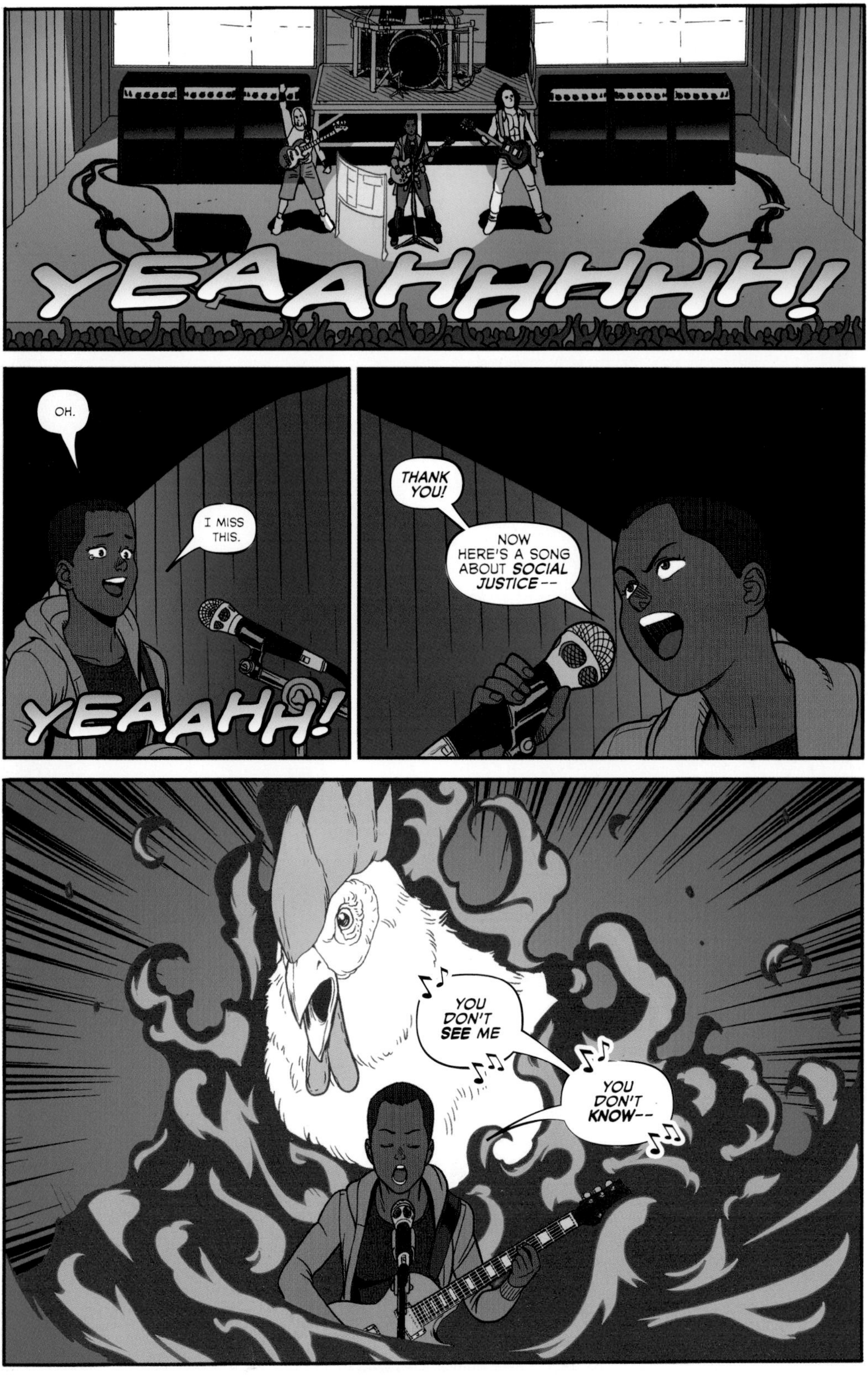
YEAAHHHHH!
OH.
I MISS THIS.
YEAAHH!
THANK YOU!
NOW HERE'S A SONG ABOUT SOCIAL JUSTICE--
YOU DON'T SEE ME
YOU DON'T KNOW--

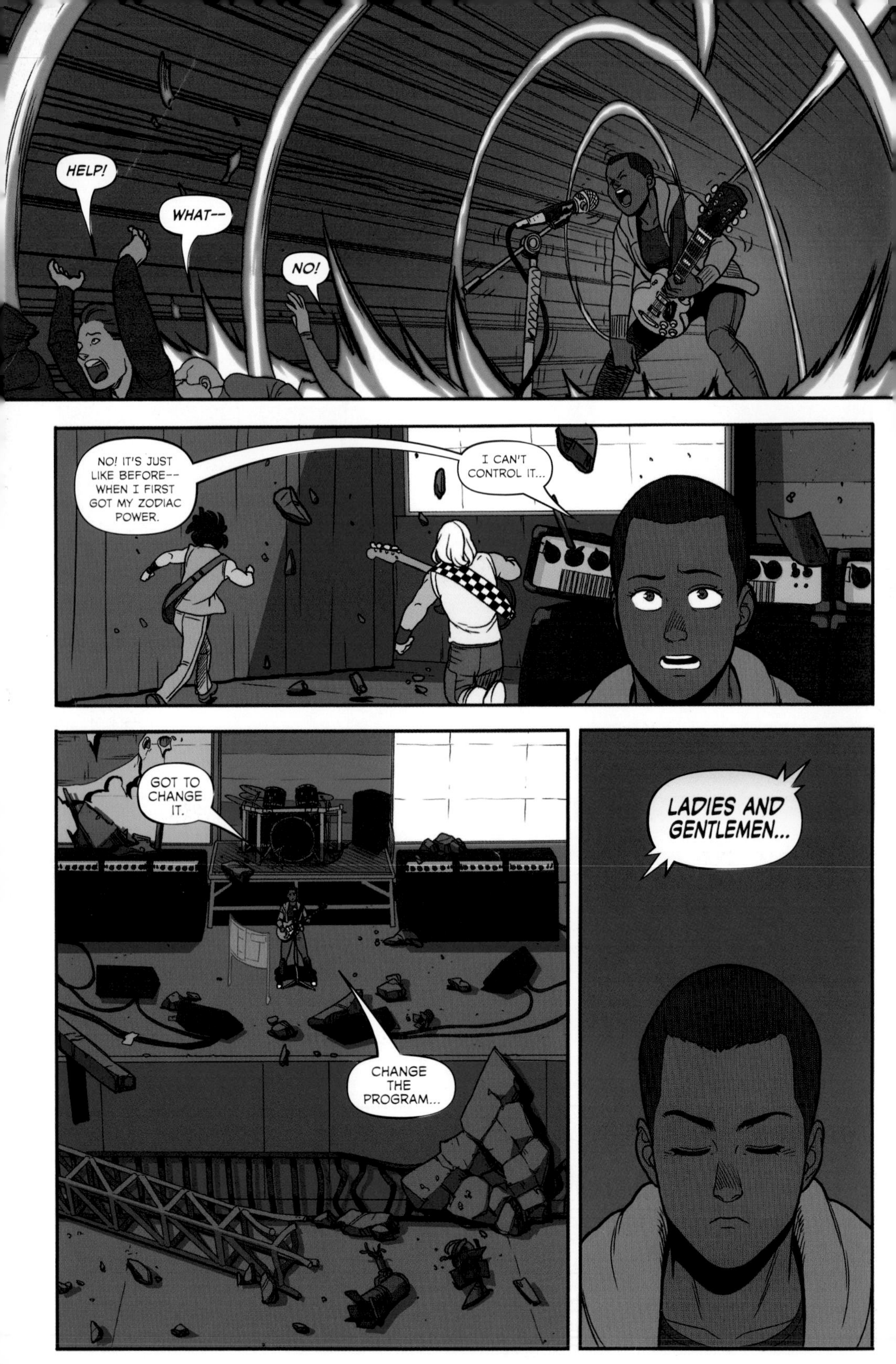
HELP!
WHAT--
NO!
NO! IT'S JUST LIKE BEFORE-- WHEN I FIRST GOT MY ZODIAC POWER.
I CAN'T CONTROL IT...
GOT TO CHANGE IT.
CHANGE THE PROGRAM...
LADIES AND GENTLEMEN...

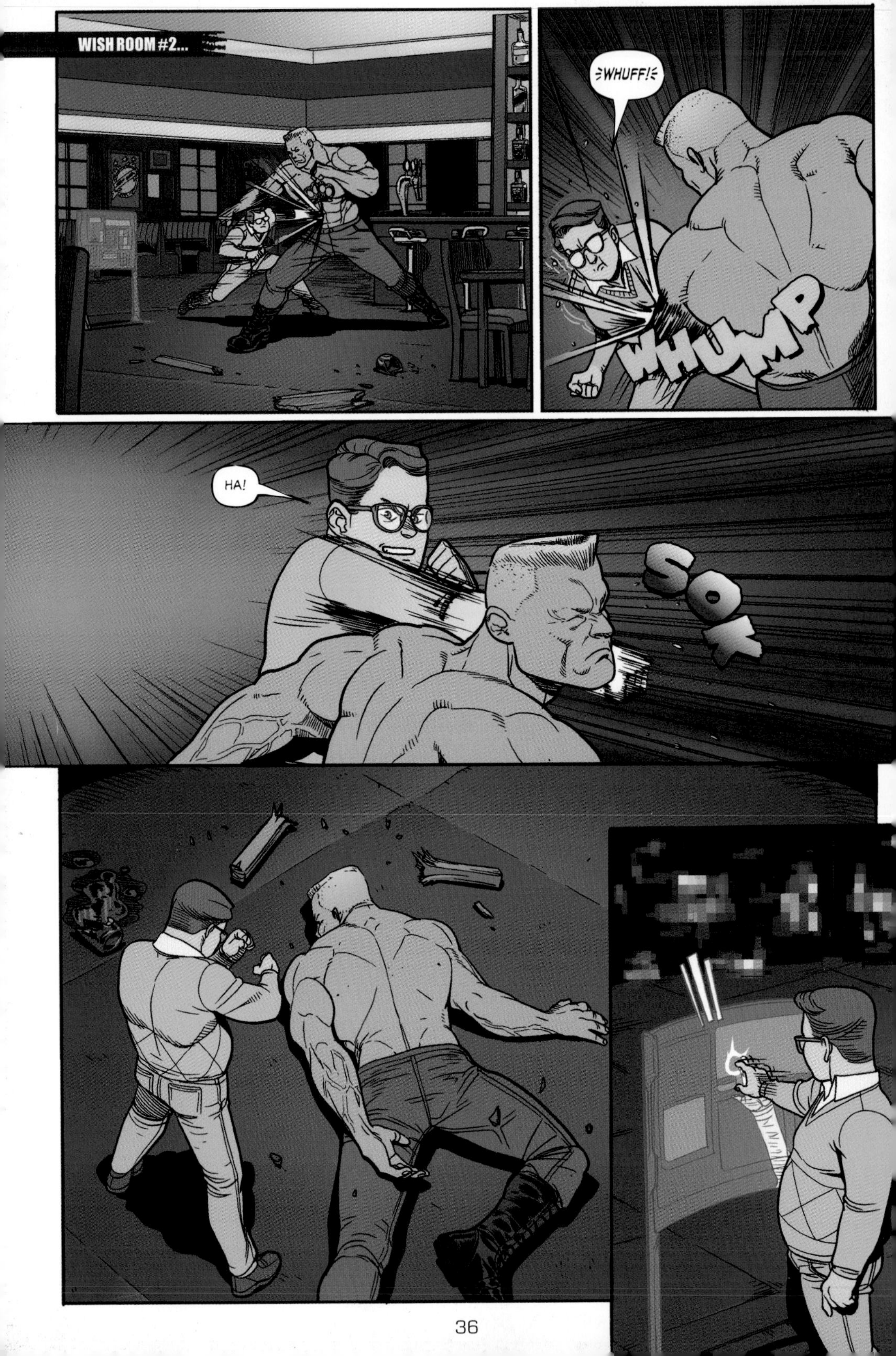
WISH ROOM #2...
WHUFF!
WHUMP
HA!
SOK

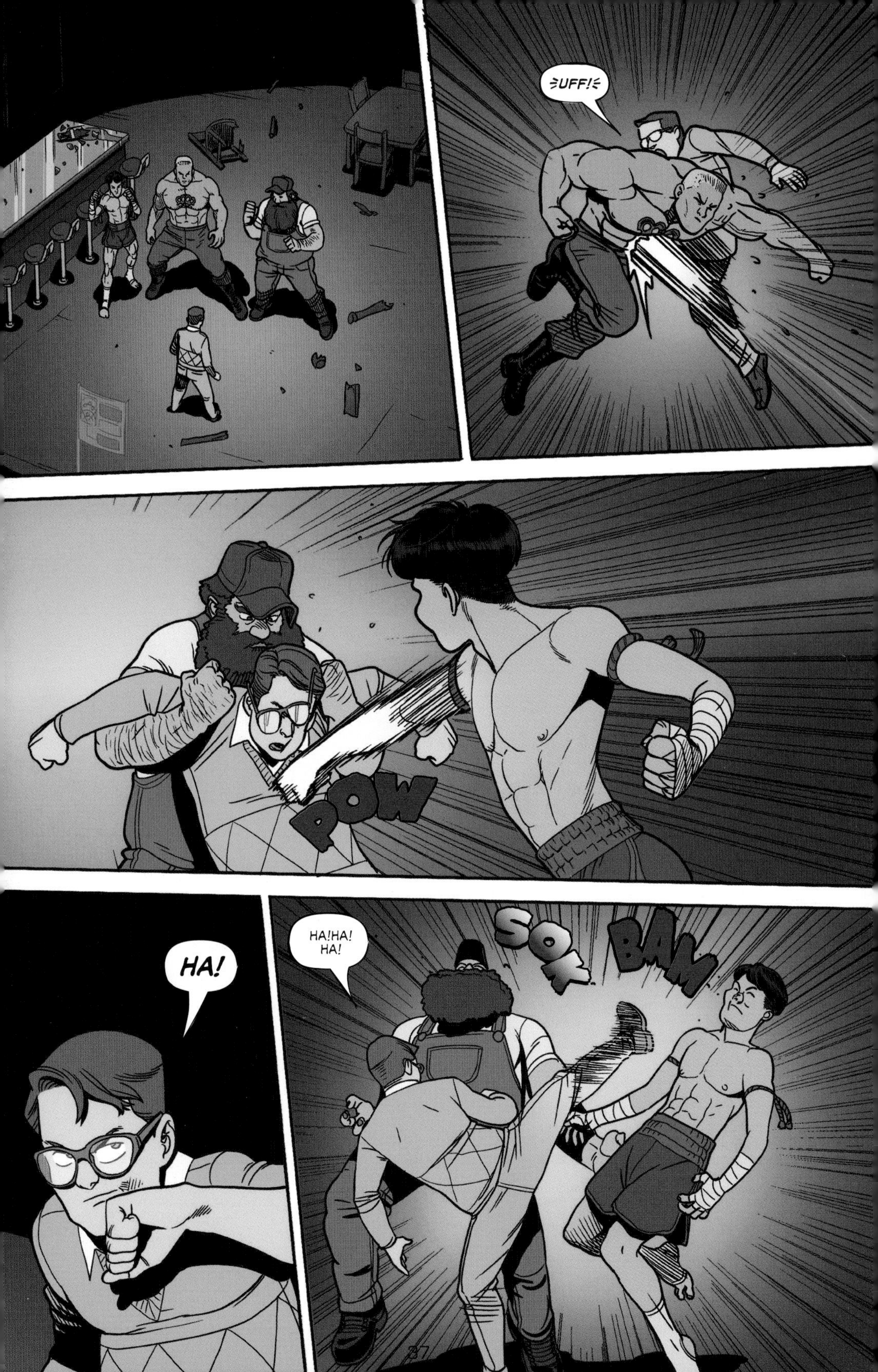
UFF!
POW
HA!
HA!HA!
HA!
SOK
BAM

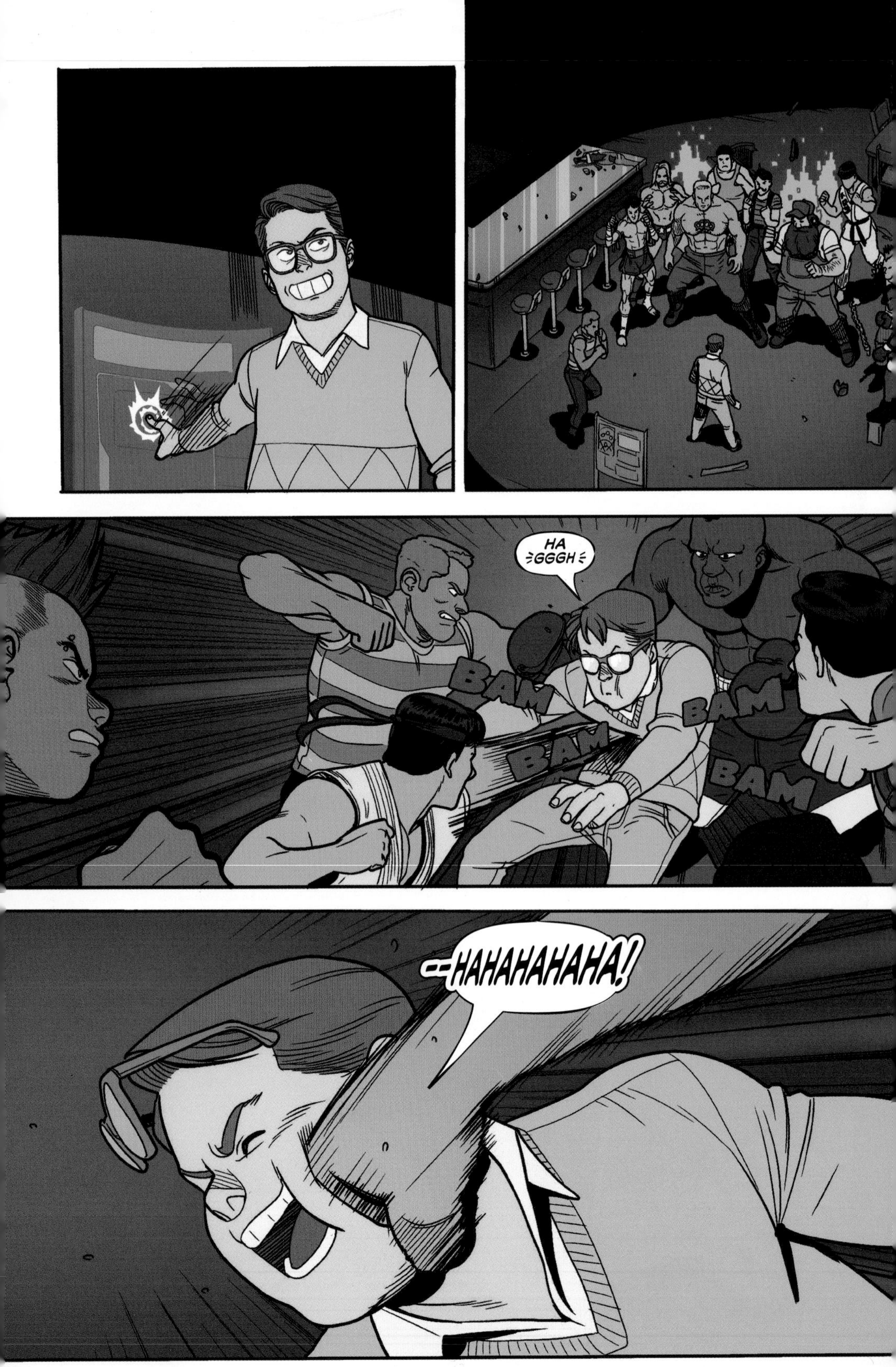
HA GGGH
BAM
BAM
BAM
BAM
--HAHAHAHAHA!

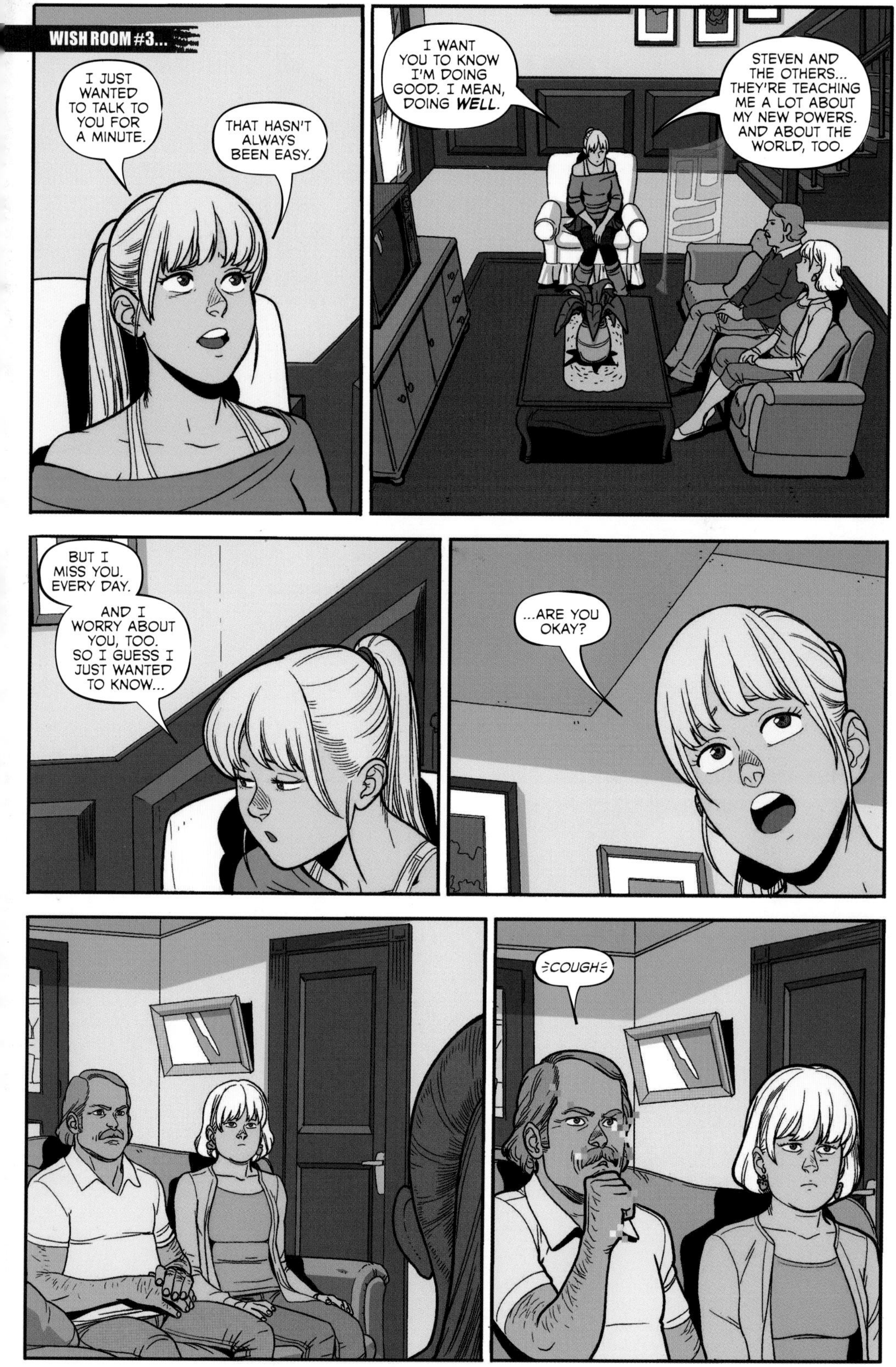
WISH ROOM #3...
I JUST WANTED TO TALK TO YOU FOR A MINUTE.
THAT HASN'T ALWAYS BEEN EASY.
I WANT YOU TO KNOW I'M DOING GOOD. I MEAN, DOING WELL.
STEVEN AND THE OTHERS... THEY'RE TEACHING ME A LOT ABOUT MY NEW POWERS. AND ABOUT THE WORLD, TOO.
BUT I MISS YOU. EVERY DAY.
AND I WORRY ABOUT YOU, TOO. SO I GUESS I JUST WANTED TO KNOW...
...ARE YOU OKAY?
COUGH

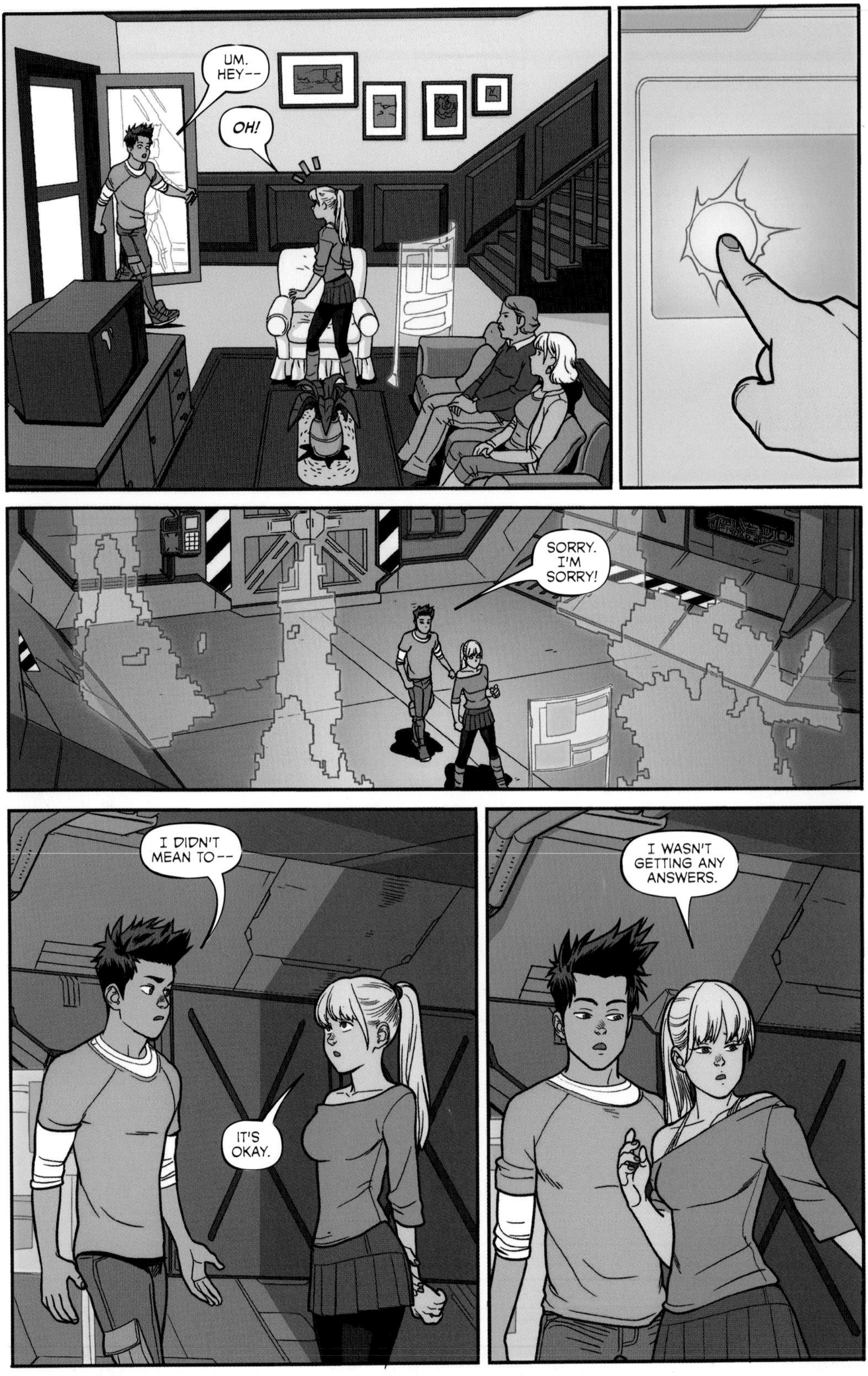
UM. HEY--
OH!
SORRY. I'M SORRY!
I DIDN'T MEAN TO--
IT'S OKAY.
I WASN'T GETTING ANY ANSWERS.

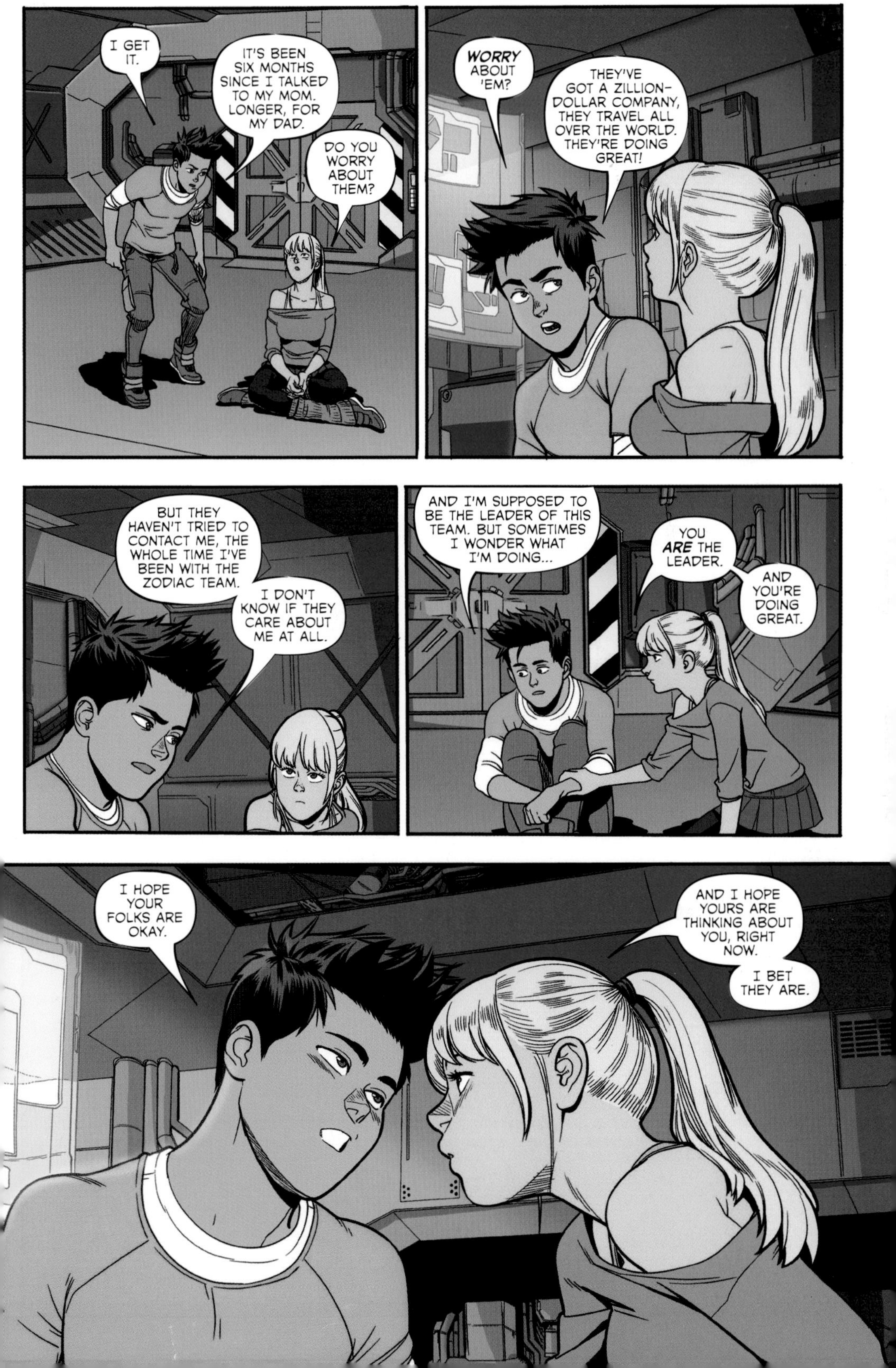
I GET IT.
IT'S BEEN SIX MONTHS SINCE I TALKED TO MY MOM. LONGER, FOR MY DAD.
DO YOU WORRY ABOUT THEM?
WORRY ABOUT 'EM?
THEY'VE GOT A ZILLION-DOLLAR COMPANY, THEY TRAVEL ALL OVER THE WORLD. THEY'RE DOING GREAT!
BUT THEY HAVEN'T TRIED TO CONTACT ME, THE WHOLE TIME I'VE BEEN WITH THE ZODIAC TEAM.
I DON'T KNOW IF THEY CARE ABOUT ME AT ALL.
AND I'M SUPPOSED TO BE THE LEADER OF THIS TEAM. BUT SOMETIMES I WONDER WHAT I'M DOING...
YOU *ARE* THE LEADER.
AND YOU'RE DOING GREAT.
I HOPE YOUR FOLKS ARE OKAY.
AND I HOPE YOURS ARE THINKING ABOUT YOU, RIGHT NOW.
I BET THEY ARE.

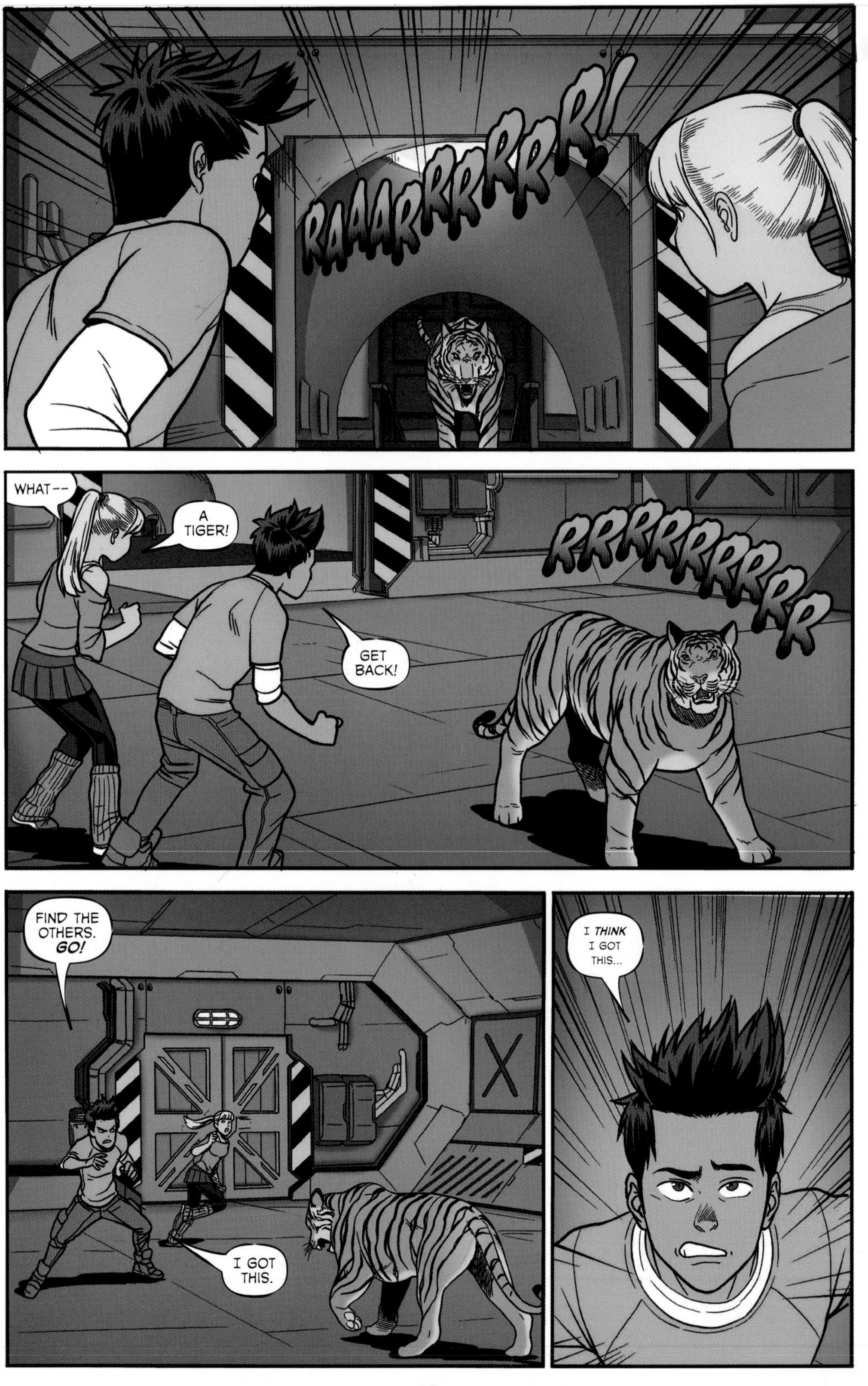
RAAARRRRRR!
WHAT--
A TIGER!
RRRRRRRRRR
GET BACK!
FIND THE OTHERS. *GO!*
I GOT THIS.
I *THINK* I GOT THIS...

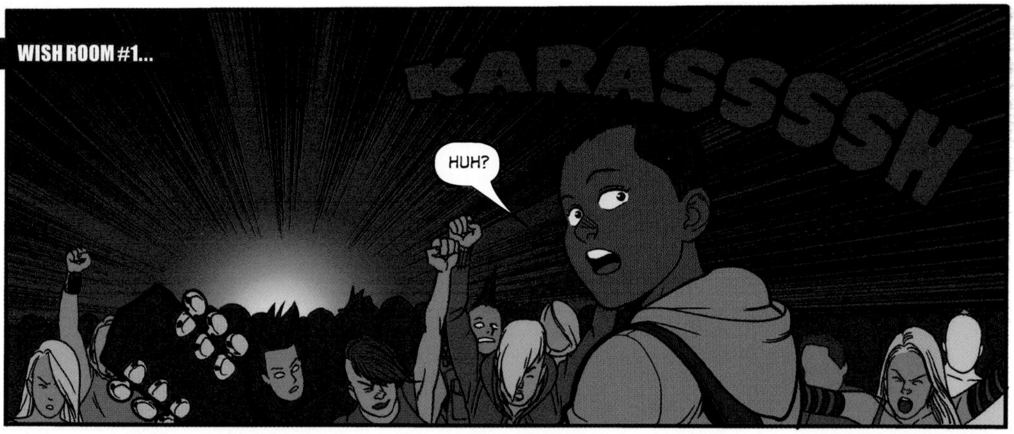
WISH ROOM #1...
KARASSSSSH
HUH?

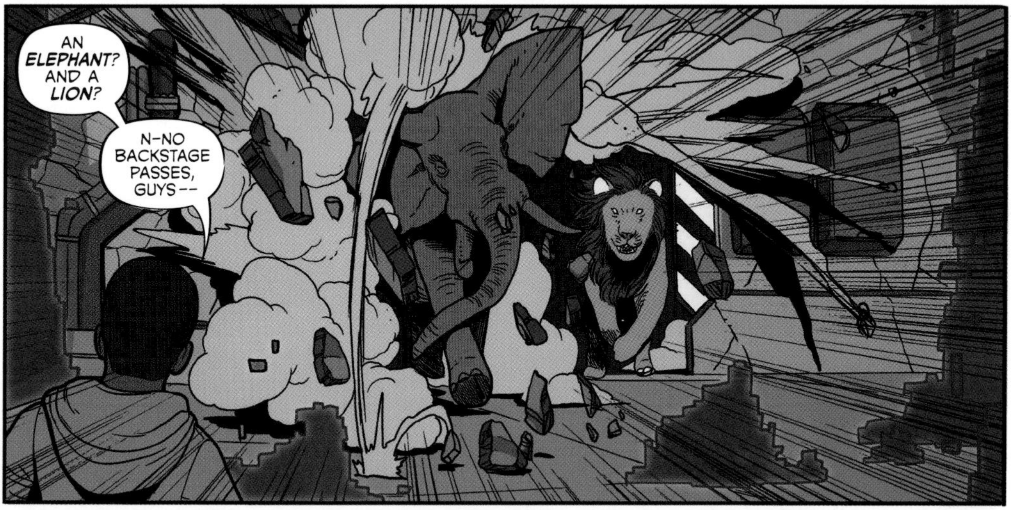
AN *ELEPHANT?* AND A *LION?*
N-NO BACKSTAGE PASSES, GUYS--

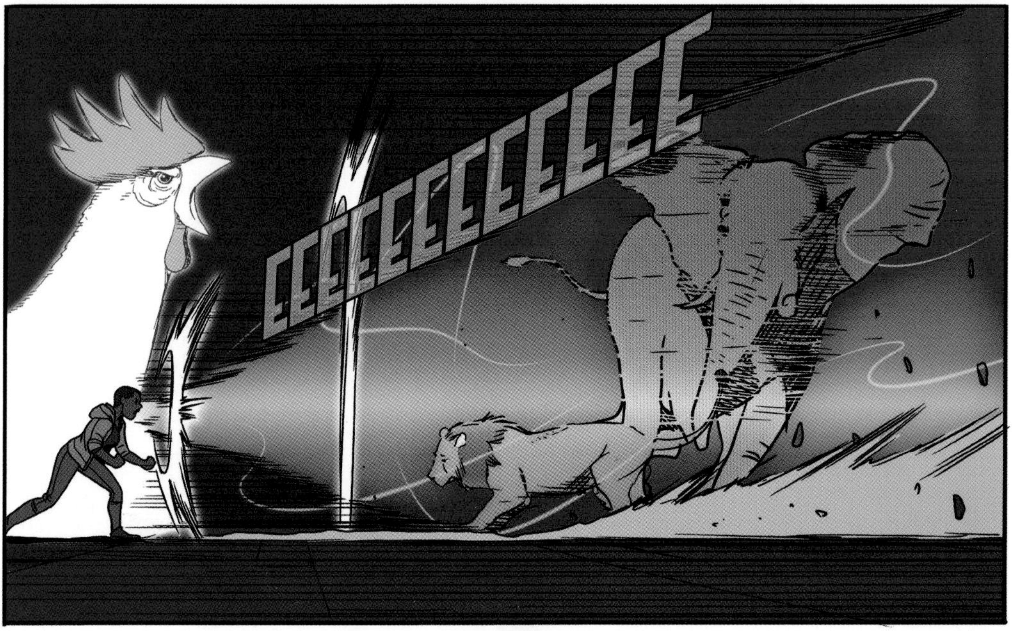
EEEEEEEEEEEEE

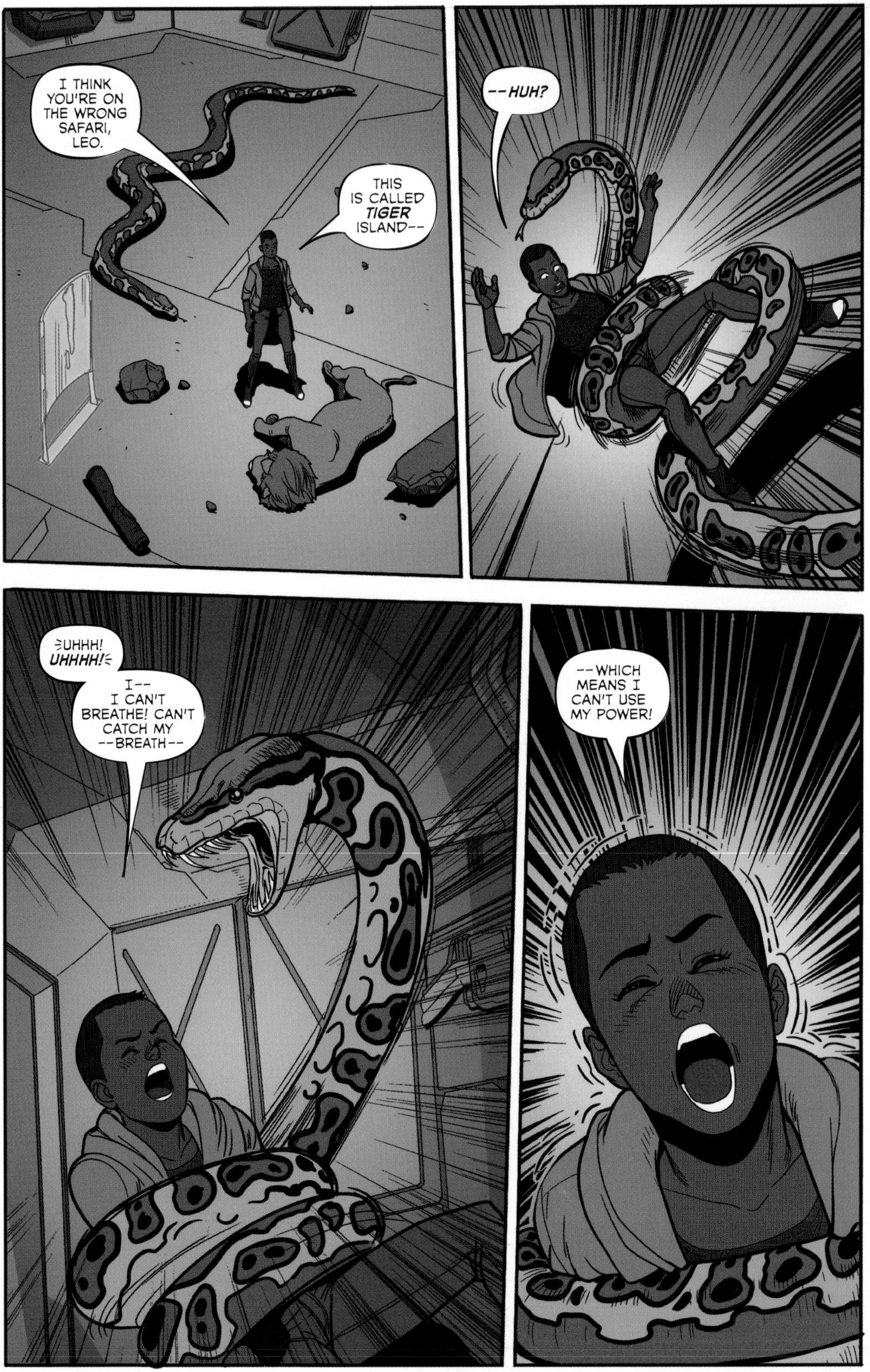
I THINK YOU'RE ON THE WRONG SAFARI, LEO.
THIS IS CALLED *TIGER* ISLAND--
--*HUH?*
UHHH! ***UHHHH!***
I-- I CAN'T BREATHE! CAN'T CATCH MY --BREATH--
--WHICH MEANS I CAN'T USE MY POWER!

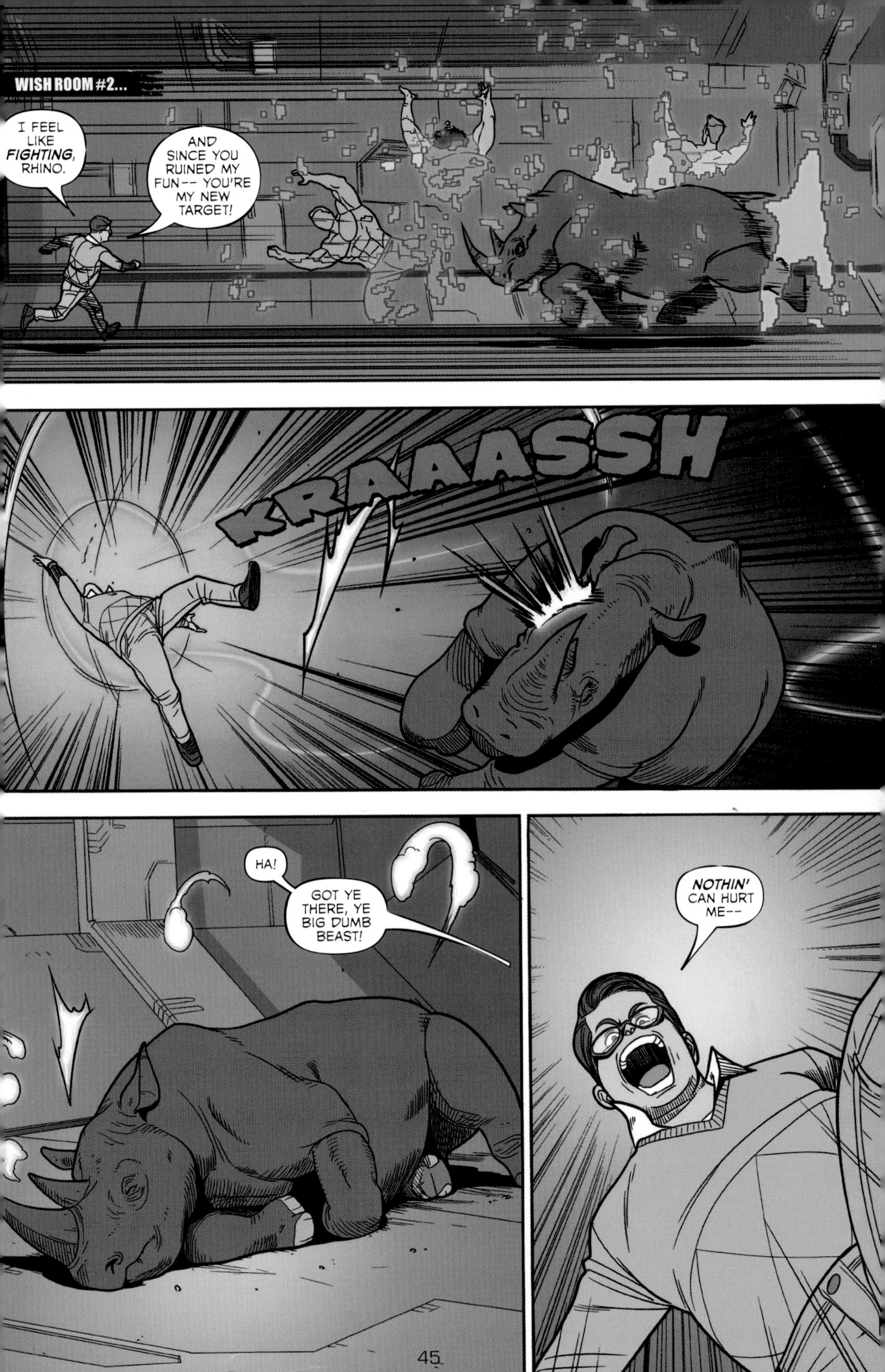

WISH ROOM #2...
I FEEL LIKE *FIGHTING*, RHINO.
AND SINCE YOU RUINED MY FUN-- YOU'RE MY NEW TARGET!
KRAAASSH
HA!
GOT YE THERE, YE BIG DUMB BEAST!
NOTHIN' CAN HURT ME--

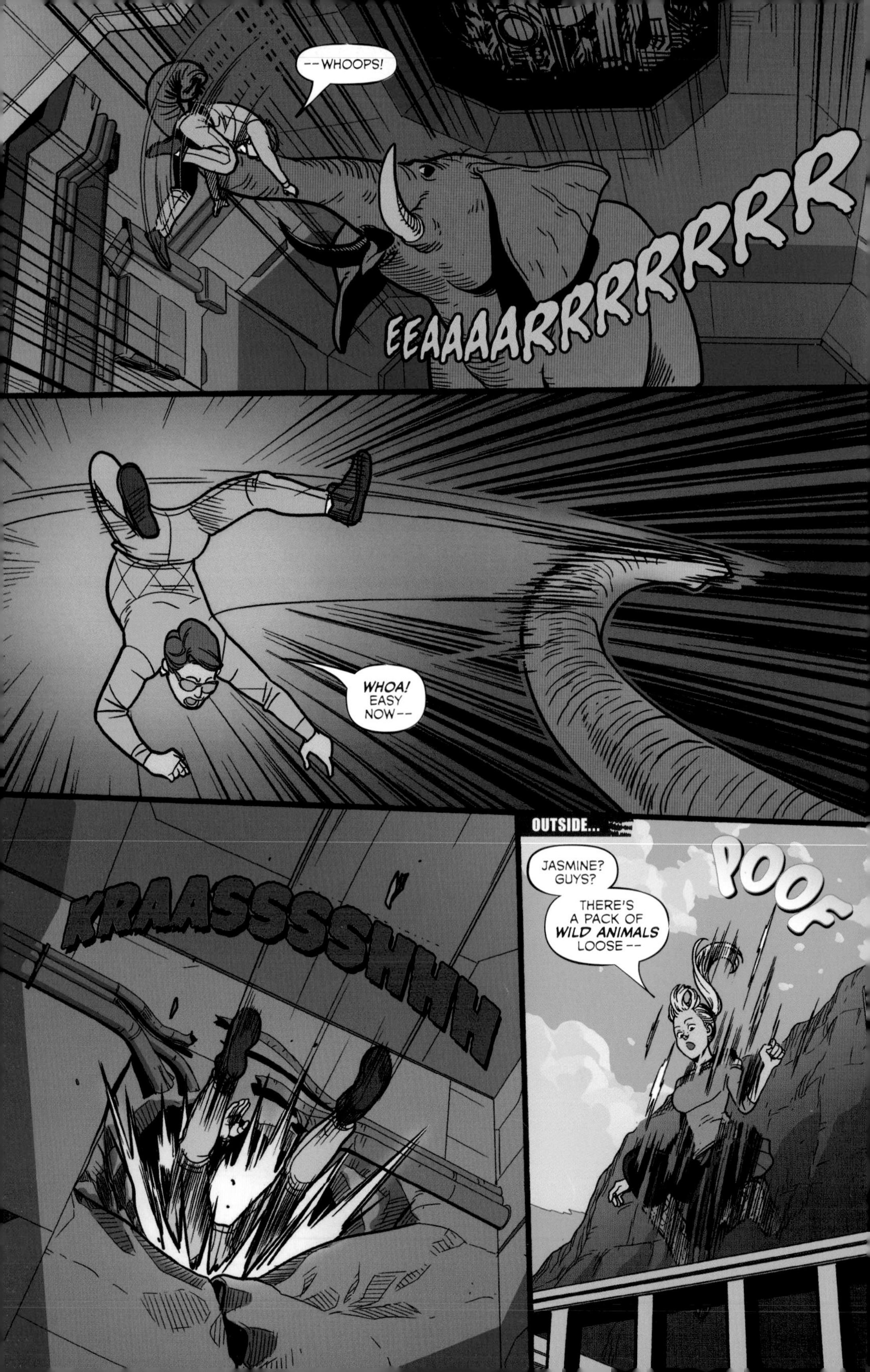
--WHOOPS!
EEAAAARRRRRRRRR
WHOA! EASY NOW--
KRAASSSSSHHH
OUTSIDE...
JASMINE? GUYS?
THERE'S A PACK OF WILD ANIMALS LOOSE--
POOF

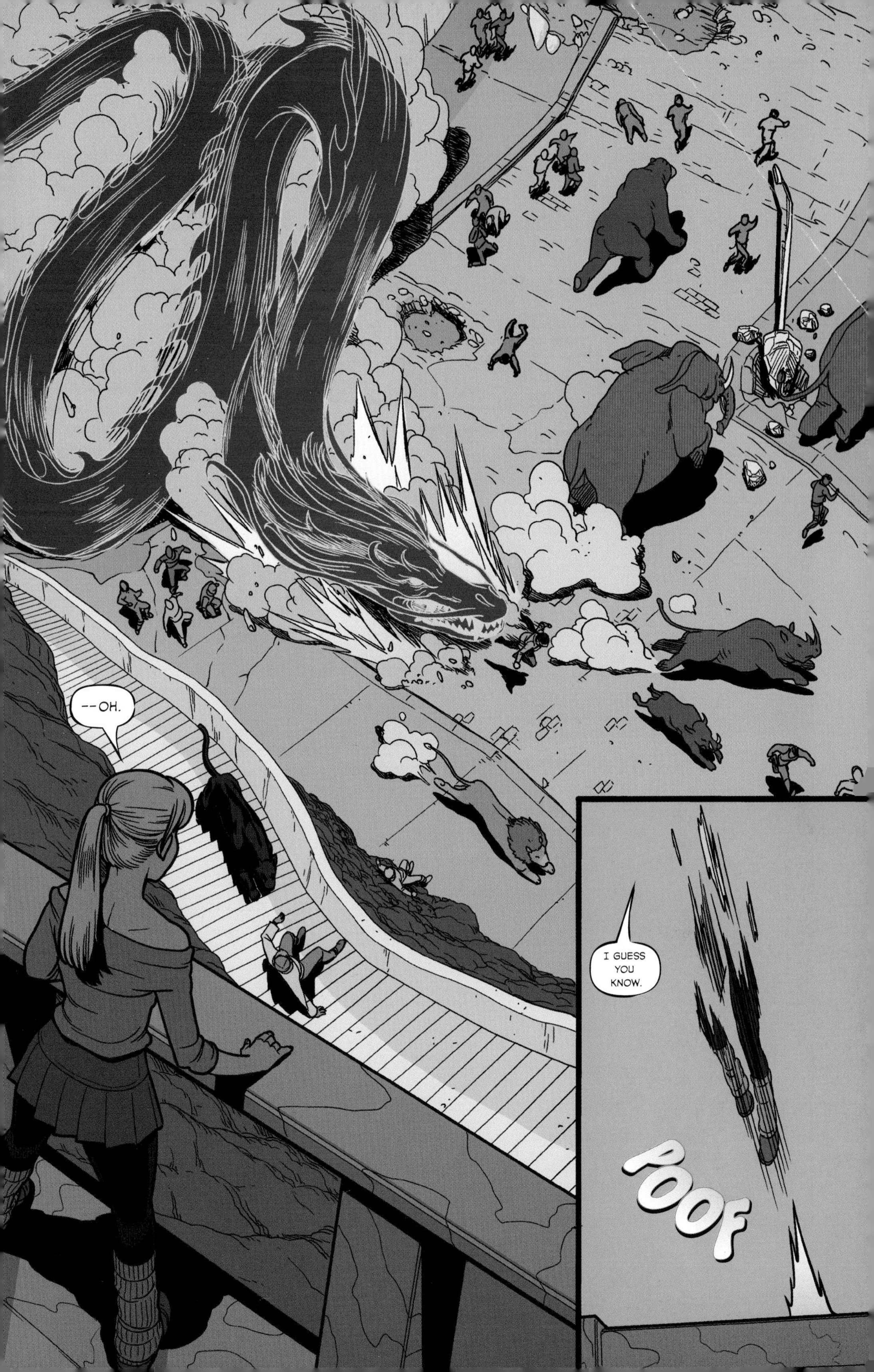
--OH.
I GUESS YOU KNOW.
POOF

48

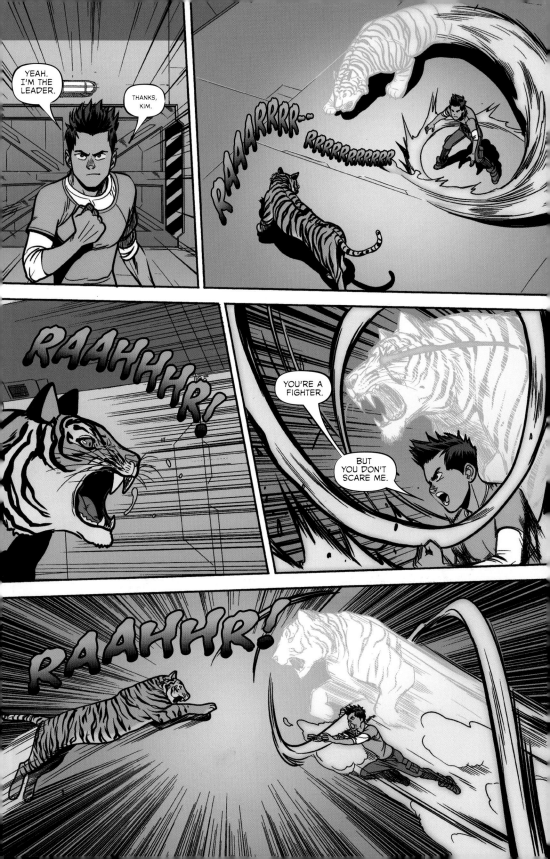

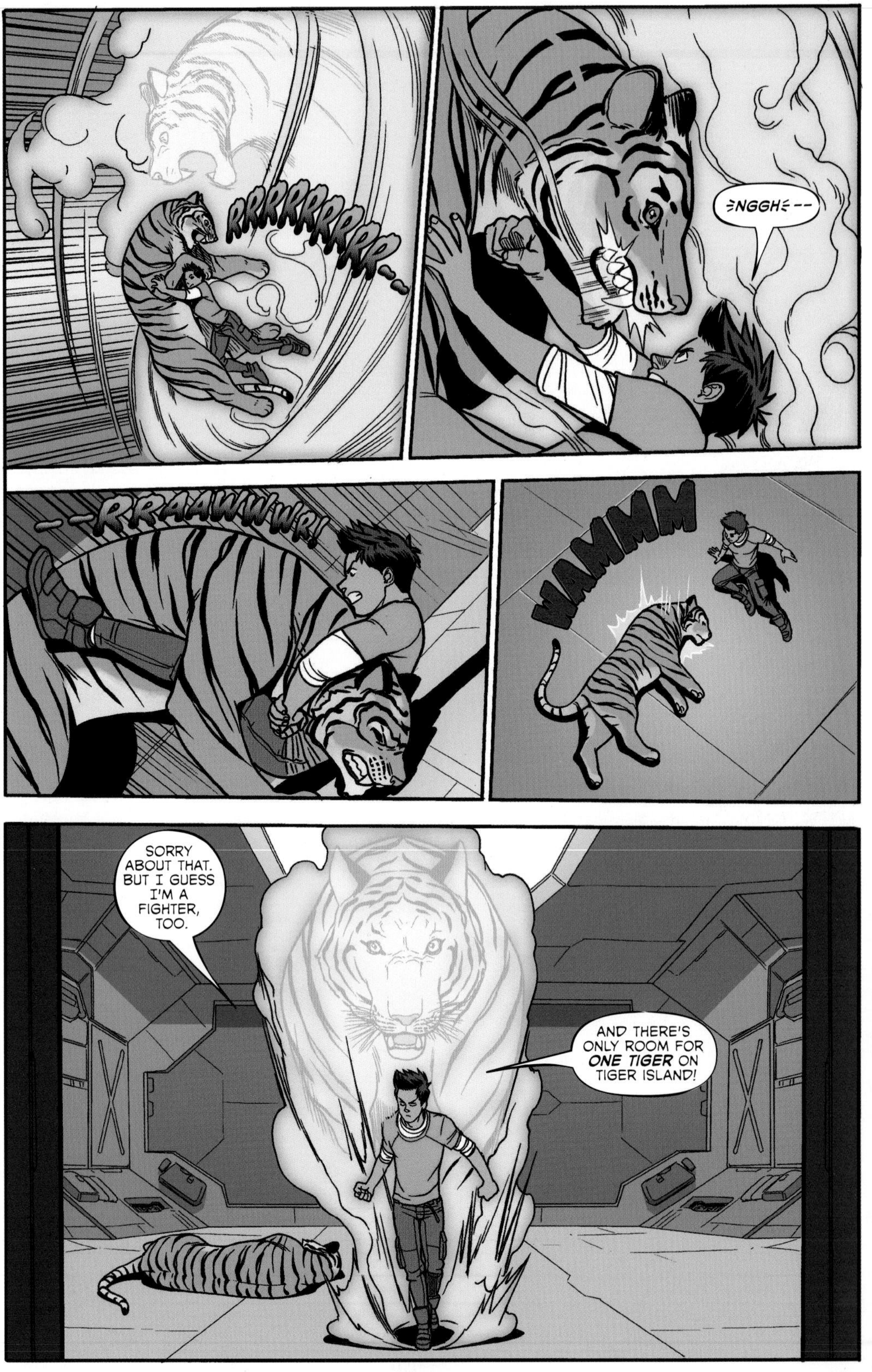
RRRRRRRRR--
NGGH--
--RRAAWWWR!
WAMMM
SORRY ABOUT THAT. BUT I GUESS I'M A FIGHTER, TOO.
AND THERE'S ONLY ROOM FOR ONE TIGER ON TIGER ISLAND!

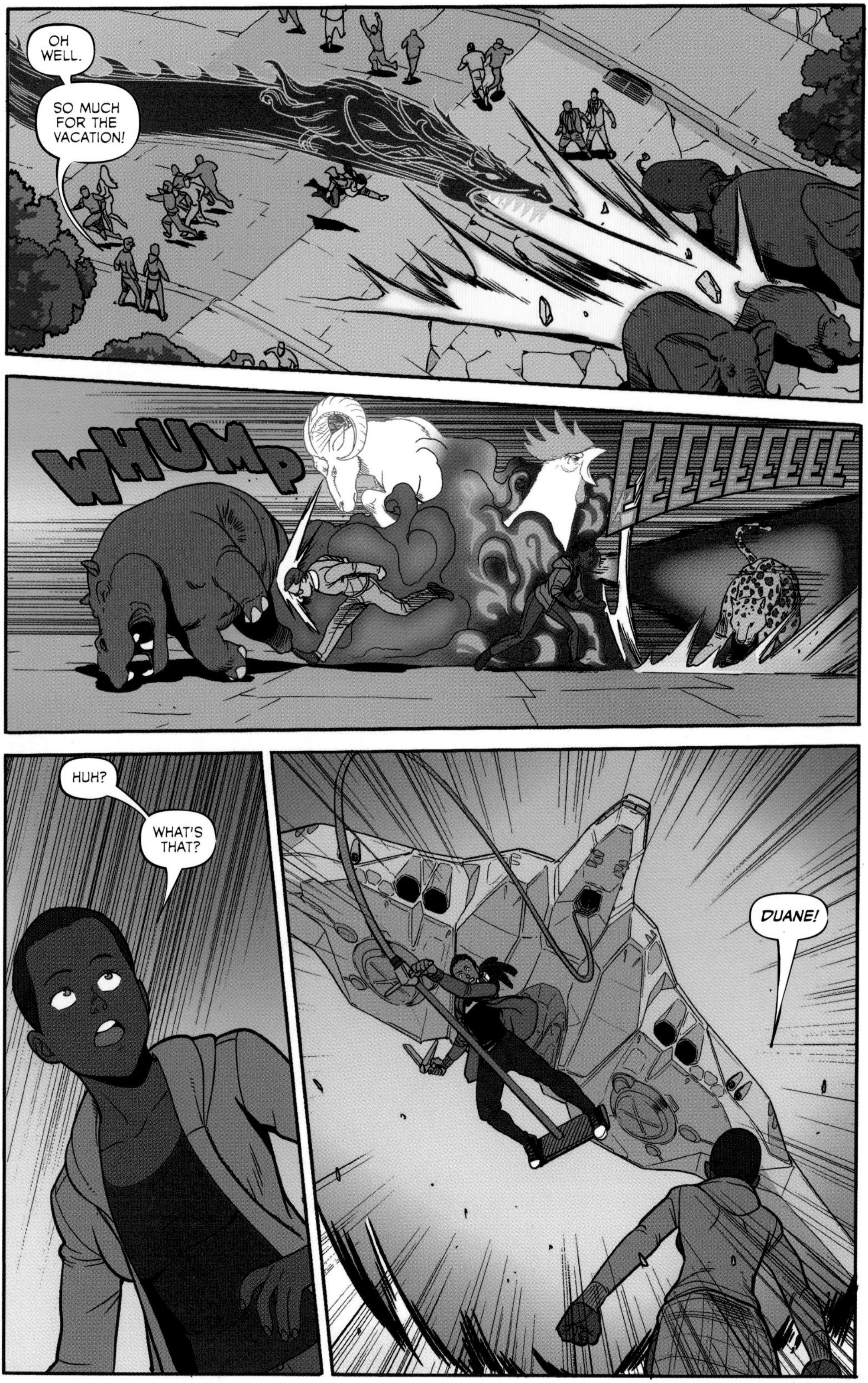
OH WELL.
SO MUCH FOR THE VACATION!
WHUMP
EEEEEEEEE
HUH?
WHAT'S THAT?
DUANE!

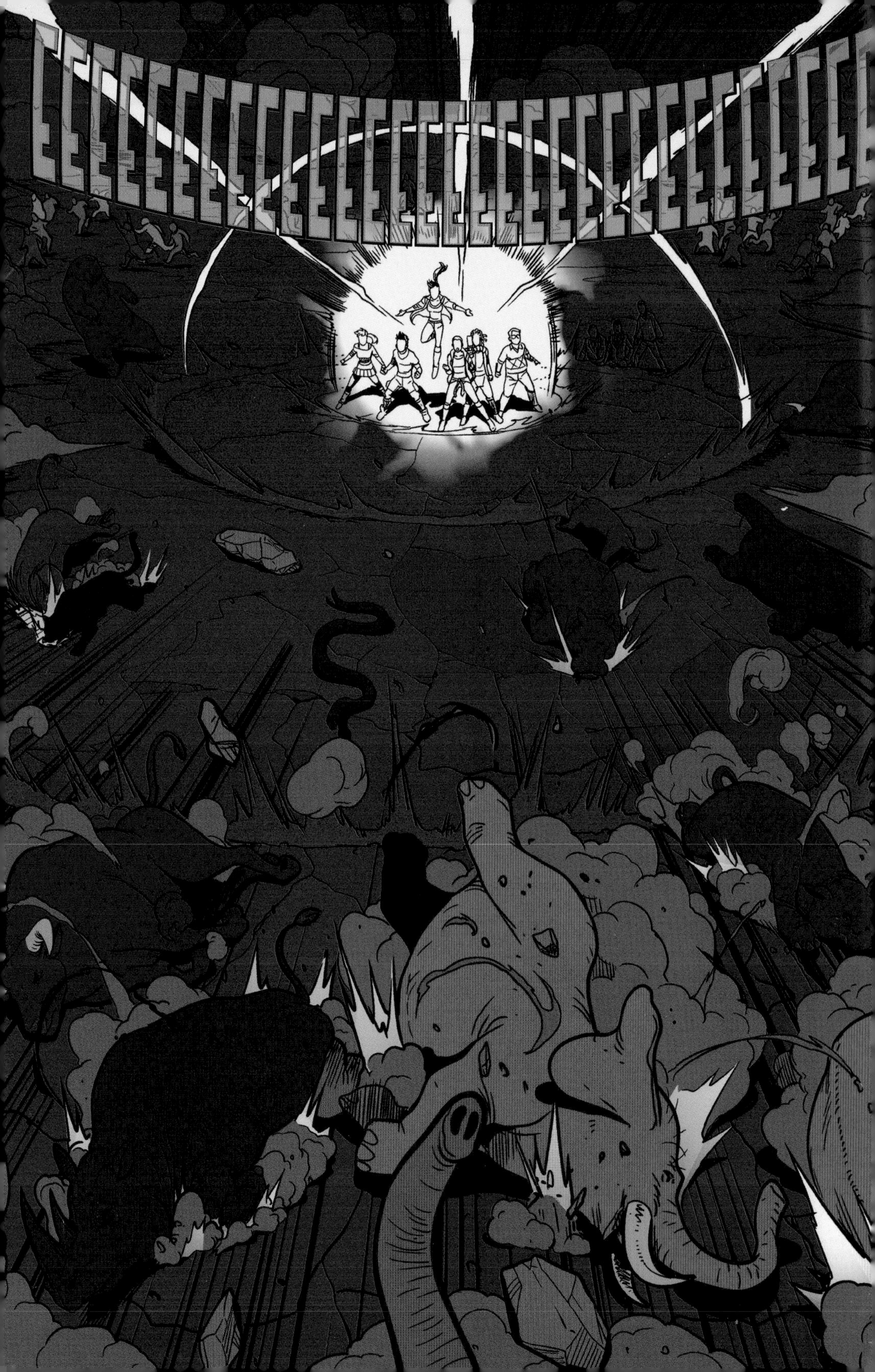
EEEEEEEEEEEEEEEEEEEEEEEEEEEEEE

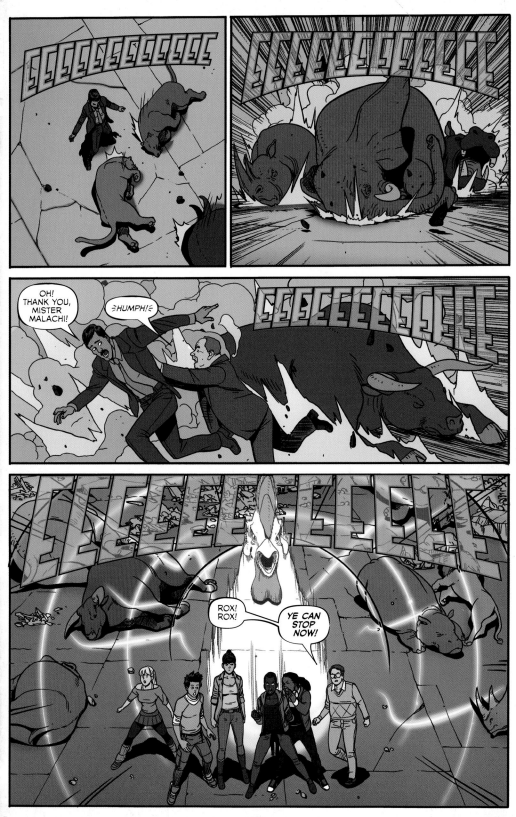

AUSTRALIA

BET YOU DIDN'T KNOW I COULD IMITATE HANDWRITING, HUH?

THAT'S NOT EVEN PART OF MY ZODIAC POWER.

JUST SOMETHING I LEARNED, BACK WHEN I USED TO FORGE CHECKS!

THANK YOU, THIAGO. YOU'VE PERFORMED SPLENDIDLY, AS ALWAYS.

THIAGO
The Rat
POWERS:
SUPERHUMAN REFLEXES, INTUITION

MAXWELL.

WELCOME BACK, CARLOS.

YOU'VE BEEN MISSED.

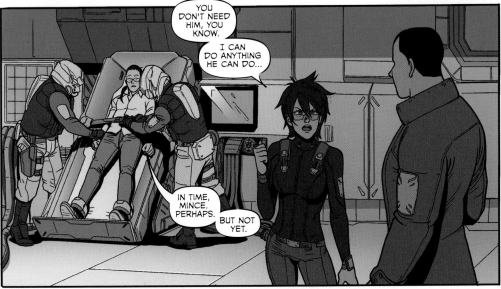

YOU DON'T NEED HIM, YOU KNOW.

I CAN DO ANYTHING HE CAN DO...

IN TIME, MINCE, PERHAPS.

BUT NOT YET.

61

WATCH OUT FOR PAPERCUTZ™

Welcome to the pulse-pounding premiere of THE ZODIAC LEGACY graphic novel series, created by Stan Lee, written by Stuart Moore, and illustrated by P.H. Marcondes, from Papercutz—those daily-horoscope-followers dedicated to publishing great graphic novels for all ages. I'm Jim Salicrup, a Gemini and a Rooster, as well as Editor-in-Chief of this little operation. I normally use this space in most Papercutz titles to offer a peek behind-the-scenes, but this time it's different.

Photo by Cherie Tieri

Jim and Stan the Man!

This time it's personal.

Growing up in the Bronx, New York, I was a big fan of all comics-- any comics I could get my hands on. And back then it wasn't all that easy—there weren't comicbook stores like there are now, libraries didn't have collections of comics, digital comics didn't even exist, and newsstand distribution was spotty at best. But still I would haunt the newsstands and any store that sold comics eagerly searching for the new releases.

Each publisher had an interesting style of their own and published great comics. One publisher that really connected with me was Marvel Comics. It was probably because its editor, Stan "the Man" Lee made such a concerted effort to speak directly to Marvel's fans on the Bullpen Bulletins page, on the Letters page, on the covers, in the footnotes in the comics, in the advertising, and especially in his column, Stan's Soapbox. It was his combination of cornball humor and tongue-in-cheek hyperbole that spoke to me. Marvel Comics characters were all "Amazing," "Fantastic," and "Incredible"! (In fact, Stan's new comics autobiography is called: Amazing Fantastic Incredible: A Marvelous Memoir.) Stan would make outrageous claims, such as calling THE FANTASTIC FOUR "The World's Greatest Comics Magazine," and actually producing a comic that arguably could be considered the World's Greatest Comics Magazine. Stan was exceptional at creating real fun and excitement around the Marvel line of comics, including its characters, creators, and "culture-loving" fans. It was so infectious, that it became my dream to one day work in the Mighty Marvel Bullpen.

And, believe it or not, at age 15, as the result of simply sending in a postcard, I wound up working within the Hallowed Halls of Marvel Comics. I was just a messenger, but I got in the front door, and stayed for twenty years, eventually becoming a writer and editor in the process. And I got to work for my idol, Stan Lee. It was a dream come true. I can't begin to tell you how much I learned by simply being in the same office as Mr. Lee (which only lasted ten years, as he moved out to Hollywood to oversee Marvel's properties move over into other media, such as cartoons, TV series, and movies). When I finally left Marvel, I thought my days of working with Stan were over. Imagine my surprise years later when I became Senior Writer/Editor at Stan Lee Media. When that was suddenly over, it was time for me and Terry Nantier to start up Papercutz. Surely, that had to be it—my days of working with my idol had to finally be over, right? Well, here we are seven years later, and we're publishing a new series of graphic novels based on characters and concepts created by Stan Lee. Who could ask for anything more? Life is good and I couldn't possibly be any happier!

STAY IN TOUCH!

EMAIL: salicrup@papercutz.com
WEB: www.papercutz.com
TWITTER: @papercutzgn
FACEBOOK: PAPERCUTZGRAPHICNOVELS
REGULAR MAIL: Papercutz, 160 Broadway, Suite 700, East Wing, New York, NY 10038

Okay, we know I love THE ZODIAC LEGACY, but now it's time for you to tell us what you think! We hope you loved it and you'll be back for THE ZODIAC LEGACY #2 "Power Line"!

Thanks,

Jim

STAN LEE
Creator

As if co-creating the Marvel Universe with such characters as Spder-Man, The Avengers, The X-Men Daredevil, The Incredible Hulk, Dr. Strange, and countless others, wasn't enough, Stan created a new generation of heroes with THE ZODIAC LEGACY!

STUART MOORE
Writer
Co-Author of THE ZODIAC LEGACY prose novels, Stuart is a writer and an award-winning comics editor.

P.H. MARCONDES
Artist
P.H. has been with Papercutz almost since the beginning illustrating such best-selling titles as THE HARDY BOYS, LEGO® NINJAGO, and SABAN'S THE POWER RANGERS.

ANDIE TONG
Cover Artist
Illustrator of THE ZODIAC LEGACY prose novel, he's a comic artist, multi-media designer, and book illustrator.